Karnov: P [illegible] er of the

By

Matthew Knight, Howie K. Bentley and Byron A. Roberts

Foreword by Jon Zaremba

Cover art by Bebeto DarOZ

ISBN 978-1-7334086-3-9

Cover design by Michael Greylord.

TABLE OF CONTENTS

Foreword

By Jon Zaremba

I've been looking at a blank page for many hours now, trying to find the right words to introduce the wonderful book that you hold in your hands. A book which I was proud to read while it was being developed and a foreword which I am honored to have been recruited to write.

I do my best to approach all significant endeavors with a relentless commitment to honesty. For better or worse, everything from the music I've recorded to the stories I've penned to the photos I've taken and to the comments I've posted... all of it has been built on a foundation of intellectual honesty that has often times hindered my potential exposure as a creator. It is with that spirit of introspective truth-telling that firstly, I am aware that you may not know who I am... and secondly I admit to not being worthy of introducing these tales of Karnov.

However, I am here. Although apprehensive, I will introduce this book to you, and do so solemnly. Perhaps in the process you will get to know me better and my inclusion here will be justified.

Being an outsider to both sword and sorcery as well as heavy metal has not detracted from my unabashed love of both. In fact, absorbing these art forms from an objective perspective has actually further fostered my adoration. I have written some blog posts for DMR, a few reviews, and done some interviews over the years too. By approaching the subject objectively, I can get deep into the philosophy behind the art that I love. I enjoy this approach because it helps me understand why a story, album, or painting has a particular effect on me.

While heavy metal was not the first, second, or even third musical love of my life, it is the type of music I hold most dearly, and that when produced correctly, is the type of music that I most identify with... because of the philosophy that is woven (sometimes subconsciously) into its fabric. I am not a metalhead. I've never been part of any sort of scene or culture. In fact, I didn't come to metal until the 1990s, much later than others my age. I grew up in a small Pennsylvania town only knowing of heavy metal peripherally. It wasn't until the dawn of the internet that I became aware of how this form of music had evolved to supremacy.

I didn't get into metal via bands like Maiden, Metallica, or Priest. I skipped the whole hair band phenomena of the 1980s. In fact, one of my first metal CDs, as gifted to me by my old friend Dale Vied, was Byron A. Roberts' BAL SAGOTH album *Starfire Burning Upon the Ice-Veiled Throne of Ultima Thule*, followed shortly thereafter by *Battle Magic*. This was my first impression of heavy metal, and ultimately sword and sorcery, for I got into that type of literature through the music. I loved both of those earlier BAL SAGOTH albums, but it was *Atlantis Ascendant* that completely blew me away. I remember the exact moment I saw it on the shelf of an independent record store in Riverside, CA. I had never seen this sort of thing for sale in person before. The inclusion of epic underground metal among the popular dreck of the early 2000s lit a fire within me that greatly influenced my creative efforts.

A few years later while living in Utah, I learned about Howie K. Bentley's CAULDRON BORN through Denis Gulbey of Sentinel Steel. *Born of the Cauldron* was my introduction to his universe, an album that not only led me to his other musical projects and literary works, but also established a friendship between us. Over the years, Howie has become one of my most trusted friends and mentors, providing guidance and advice that has helped to improve my own writing. Like most other artists who are beautifully prolific in their depiction of true darkness and carnage, Howie is a genuinely polite and thoughtful fellow.

It was through Howie that I came to know Matthew Knight. I was in need of a guest narrator for my final album *Promontory*. I was disheartened by the lackluster responses I was receiving from the ads I had circulated. I explained to Howie that I wanted someone who would appreciate my short story around which the album was composed, someone who would perform the lines theatrically with passion and conviction. Matthew was the first person that Howie recommended. To this day, there is nobody I would have rather included in the punctuation of my era as a musician than Matthew Knight. He played the role of Mark Oberheim on the album, providing a heartfelt performance. I quickly fell in love with his band ETERNAL WINTER and we also sparked a great friendship that led to other collaborations including our sound-novel project HAUNTED ABBEY MYTHOS.

Traditionally, a foreword is included as a means to validate the work of the author. The three monoliths who have joined forces to bring you *Karnov* do not need any validation, let alone mine. I view Matthew, Howie, and Byron as friends, mentors, and heroes. At best, and even this is a stretch… I'm a Wrathmane to their Karnov. "Who is Wrathmane?" you ask… you're soon to find out.

For what you are about to read is a thrilling story that spans multiple worlds and includes several intriguing heroes and villains. These two stories of Karnov are full of supernatural horror, intense gore, and epic battles… tales that are born from the true fundamentals of heavy metal as expressed by three authors who have lived and breathed heavy metal during the decade of cultural betrayal. In addition to their metal esthetics, these two books of Karnov also contain a few moments of well-placed humor, sometimes less obviously than others, but always making these stories legitimately fun to read.

Part of what makes this book fun is that each author takes turn telling a chapter of the story, a technique that I didn't think would work until I actually read it. Each of their individual voices is clearly represented by their writing style, but not at expense of the narrative itself. This adds another level to the journey that you'll take with Karnov, traversing not only the parallel worlds of his universe, but also the parallel minds of Knight, Bentley, and Roberts.

So, albeit with some trepidation as an outsider, but with the self-righteous impudence as an artist, I am honored to present to you *KARNOV: PHANTOM-CLAD RIDER OF THE COSMIC ICE!*

Karnov: Phantom-Clad Rider of the Cosmic Ice

Episode I
The Eye of Orlock

Book I
By Matthew Knight

Chapter I
A Grim Homecoming (Black is the Blood of the Night)

The sky was grayer than axe-beaten steel as I rode through the grim countryside of Duros Zuil. The dusty road I had been following for days now lead me into a familiar farmland, wreathed in fog and shadow. Surrounded by neighboring villages, it was set between brooding woods and a mass of towering black crags. A chill wind gusted through the brown, grassy hills that overtook the land, howling between skeletal branches of dead oak trees in its wake. Shady, poverty-stricken villagers tended wheat and barley fields, many of whom looked away in fear or gave unwelcoming glances when I rode past. As gloomy as the sight of this place was, for me it was a joy to behold, as it meant my journey was coming to an end. My home was in a village just beyond this land.

The battle at Orobos Sandus had left me weary. I fought hard and took many lives for the Dark Queen, Leandra, whose army clashed with that of Suntha Guull only weeks ago. The old sorcerer offended the Queen by sending numerous ineffable supernatural horrors into her territory, slaying many of her most valuable officers, while kidnapping several of the kingdom's royal maidens. These women were held captive and used in rituals within Guull's walls. At length, after fighting our way through his ranks of otherworldly creatures, we stormed the citadel, took the wizard by force, then had his head spitted on an iron stake before Leandra's throne. Now, after all the madness of battle, I was anxious to return to my wife's loving embraces and the sound of my son's joyful laughter.

Light chain mail jingled beneath my torn traveler's cloak, and my dark mane blew wildly in the sweeping gales. As I rode, I looked up to behold a baleful sight in the distance which was another symbol of home to my eyes; atop the jagged crags, brooding over this land, stood Castle Thornhaven. A sinister spectacle of black towers and battlements piercing the dark clouds above, it stood on the highest of those fearsome peaks.

A magical spell had been cast upon the mountain range—a treacherous barrier of surging red lightning existed, so that no man may climb the ridge without being destroyed. Thus, it was told that the only way the inhabitants had come to the castle was by means of sorcery.

The estate was once owned and occupied by Lord Archonea. Being empty and abandoned for a score of years, the castle was now said to have been haunted by ghosts of those who once lived there. Its huge, gaping windows stared at me like black phantom eyes as I gazed at the mighty fortress. Many times had I dazedly looked upon its dark majesty while traveling through this land, but never felt so at peace to see it as I did this day.

The trail began to rear up a rather steep hill where the farmland thinned. When my black steed Wrathmane and I neared the top we came to a more barren stretch of ashen land, which I also recognized. There were small cottages in the distance, all appearing to have their doors and windows boarded up. This seemed strange to me, as there were often commoners outside, herding livestock as their wives tended gardens and barreled water from wells. Never before had I seen the place so desolate.

Reaching the top of the slope, I came upon a clearing bestrewn with tombstones and freshly-made graves in a large area surrounded by a crude, wooden fence. It was here that the path ran through and I found myself in a queer, newly-founded graveyard. This was unfamiliar to me, as I had been through this land many times and always it had been an empty, grassy space where local children would gather and play. Something horrible must have happened while I was away and I felt uneasy as I surveyed the dreary scene.

Hungry ravens perched upon the dead trees on each side and cawed as if in mockery of my dread. From my mount, I tried to read some of the names etched into the shale and granite headstones. I recognized many of them to be people I knew from these surrounding hamlets, as well as some of my home town. This disturbed me even more.

As I neared the final rows, there were some larger tombs and sepulchers. To my surprise, from behind one of these, stepped a short figure. It was a young maiden, probably fifteen or sixteen years of age. Her wet, tangled locks were dark brown and her face seemed pale as a corpse. She wore a faded blue dress which was torn and more disintegrated than the gear I had worn in recent battle. She stared at me blankly, not moving as I came closer. I urged Wrathmane to a halt and addressed the sad, ill-looking lass.

"Hail, girl. Tell me, what tragedy was it that brought about the need for a yard such as this? For it was not here when I passed through last."

She remained silent and continued her blank gaze.

"Was there a plague or famine amongst the townsfolk?"

At this, she took a step back as if frightened, and crouched behind one of the tombstones, still leering at me eerily.

I looked at her closer and longer. Finally, I recognized the dame to be Yashanalla, fair daughter of Jondar Barthule, one of the more wealthy farmers of this poor land. I had spoken with her several times in the past when buying eggs and dried meat at the local market. She was always a kind and sweet maid with plenty to say and a pretty smile upon her face, but with her skin so filthy and her countenance in such a state as this, I barely could tell she was Barthule's lovely daughter.

Seeing as the girl was frightened, I stepped down, dismounting from my horse, and crouched to her level.

"Ah, young Yashanalla... Now I can see who you are. It is I,

Karnov, remember? I am surprised to find you this far from your home in a place such as this. Have you lost your way?"

Yashanalla looked deeply into my eyes. She appeared to be ravaged with grief, sorrow, and a strange sickness. Her face was pallid and tinged with a greenish hue. Tears welled in her bloodshot blue eyes which had dark circles beneath them. Slowly, the girl began walking toward me, arms outstretched as if longing for a comforting embrace. She reached out for me, and I pulled her into my arms.

"There, there, my child. There's no need to fret. If you are lost or somehow separated from your family, I will see to it that you are brought safely home. For your father's acreage is just down the road beyond that grove there. Don't you remember?"

Her body trembled and she sobbed as I held her close, stroking her long hair in a loving manner. Gradually, she moved her hands up to my shoulders. I continued my attempt to comfort her, as the girl was obviously upset and terribly traumatized for some reason. Her crying stopped for a moment, and she slyly moved her head so that her face was closer to my neck.

Suddenly, Yashanalla gripped my shoulders tightly, alarming me. Her head reared back and I looked up to see two huge fangs elongate from her mouth. Her eyes widened and she made a sort of hissing sound as she violently attempted to bite down into my throat. Just before her fangs could pierce my flesh, I quickly threw her from me and tumbled across the ground, drawing my sword as I arose.

The girl was up on her feet in an instant and immediately lunged toward me. Her body hit me with a force uncanny for one her size. I was knocked down and rolled with her across the dirt road until we hit a row of graves. There we wrestled, her in a state of frenzied bloodlust, and me struggling for my life. None of Suntha Guull's horrors I had faced in battle were as strong as this child, and nothing I could do would overpower her.

Yashanalla was on top of me, hissing and thrashing about, trying to once again get a clear shot at sinking teeth into my veins. Her eyes were terrible and insane-looking as venomous drool dripped from her deadly fangs. I saw an opportunity and struck her a blow to the face, just hard enough to barely knock her off me.

Quick as lightning, I leaped aside and raced to where my sword had fallen. Once again armed, I stood, ready to face another attack. She arose from the ground and shrieked madly as blood dripped from her mouth where I had struck her. Wailing like a banshee, she ran toward me, arms outstretched, ready to feast upon my mortal being. I knew what I had to do. I readied myself and the moment she came near enough, swung my sword with all my might. The blade hit home, severing through the girl's neck. Blood sprayed out, painting gray tombstones red as the head of Yashanalla toppled to the earth, rolling like a ripened gourd at Autumn Solstice.

The body lay still in a vermillion pool. I stood catching my breath and trying to come to a realization of what had just happened. Indeed there must be some horrible sorcery at work here in this land that turns young ladies into undead monstrosities such as this. I sheathed my sword and walked over to my horse that was patiently waiting. Before mounting, I looked about—still no trace of anyone in sight, and no sound other than the crows' mocking laughter.

Chapter II
Scars of Treachery (An Oath of Vengeance)

Hastening to return to my family, I came to a place where the road ended and dark woodland began. It was there that I had to travel through, as my hometown lay just beyond, on the other side of the thick woods. There were many stories about this forest and it was said to be haunted by werewolves. I myself had had few encounters with anything supernatural here, but there were always shrill cries sounding in the distance and an eerie fog engulfing the trees.

I rode along a path that continued on where the road had stopped. The thick foliage overhead caused weird shadows to dance among the antique boughs and a screech owl shrieked, announcing the coming of night.

As the path wound, I saw a small hut just up ahead with black smoke pouring from its chimney. I knew it to be the abode of D'vartha, the mysterious witch who inhabited the forest. Many people of this land shun her as only an insane woman who prefers the company of forest beasts. Others claim she has awful powers and is extremely dangerous. I myself had witnessed a few weird things when passing by and she always struck up a conversation, usually attempting to lure me into various schemes of witchcraft or sexual intimacy. On a few occasions she had succeeded...

As I approached, D'vartha was kneeling outside the hovel, tending a garden of incandescent plants and herbs that seemed to move of their own accord as she touched them. She did not look up from her work as she acknowledged my coming.

"Greetings, Karnov. How did the battle fare?"

"Greetings, witch," I replied as I urged my mount to stop briefly. "I'm afraid I have no time for you today. I must be moving on."

D'vartha stood and turned to face me. She wore a stained and ragged tightly-fitting white dress. Long crimson hair framed her pale face and fell down to her sleekly curved body. Her countenance was fair and dark lines lay beneath her emerald-colored eyes that blazed wildly. The wench always portrayed a slight appearance of madness, but she was beautiful to me in a strange way.

"Ah, I can sense bitterness in your voice," she said. "What ails you, warrior? Surely whatever it is, I can be of help."

"What do you know of the newly-made gravesite over yonder hill?" I asked. "It was not there when I departed. And why are all the houses boarded up?"

"What I know is that there has been evil at work in these lands during the past weeks that you have been gone." The enchantress smirked. "Much evil indeed... You know of the castle upon the mountaintop?"

"You mean the old Thornhaven estate? Of course..."

"Then just as those foolish goat herders, you have also believed it to have been abandoned for many years. Well, that is a myth... You see, it has been discovered that unbeknown to us, the ancient manor has had a new occupant for quite some time. Lord Ghormanteia from the northern Isle of Aschorzotha has claimed the stronghold as his own. It is now ruled by him and his servants. He is an undead sorcerer and a master of the Isle's secret black magic arts. Lately, there have been a number of vampyric wraiths invading the villages and feasting upon the blood of the townsfolk, turning them into undead creatures of which you may have encountered since your arrival."

She raised her eyebrows and looked at me with a questioning expression as she said this. I returned her gaze but said nothing.

"The unfortunate victims of these vampyres become servants of Ghormanteia," she continued as she poured water from a jug onto her plants, which made an eerie sighing sound as their roots drank. "These fiends are powerful, and believe me, they have feasted well on these boroughs since you have been away."

"How far have they invaded?" I asked.

"As it appears to me, they have ravaged the whole countryside and beyond. They are a powerful breed and there is no limit to where they can spread their wickedness."

As she spoke, I looked down at the voluptuous curves revealed by her form-fitting, frayed garment, and thought to myself that there was something else I'd like to spread… Quickly I shook my head, ridding this thought from my mind, though my eyes still lingered.

"I must hasten," I said and was about to urge Wrathmane into full gallop.

D'vartha stopped me by placing her hand on my knee.

"Karnov, wait!" she said urgently. "There is something that can be done. The people are living in fear and dying daily by the fangs of these beasts. They need someone with the ability to defeat the dark magic who will bring an end to this carnage. I can grant you that power if you will let me help you."

"I've told you before woman, I want no part in your unholy schemes of witchcraft!"

"Listen to me!" she pleaded. "This is no trick. You are the only one in this land with the strength and will who may be able to destroy a menace such as this. Through my secret arts, I can bestow upon you the means to do so."

"I must get back to my family," I said as I lifted the reins.

"Fool!" spat the witch. "The time will come when you will return to me, Karnov. And then you'll beg for what I offer. You shall see!"

Without replying, I spurred my steed, which reared as we sped off, galloping down the path. Turning my head once and looking back, through a cloud of dust I saw D'vartha staring after me with a malign smirk upon her wanton lips. She then laughed and resumed tending to her garden.

* * *

A changeling-birthing full moon shone like an evil eye over the land. By its light I finally came to the dusty, night-clad streets of my home town. Things here were just as they were in the other villages. All the houses were either boarded up or abandoned. There were no signs of life and a sense of panic struck me as I began to fear for my loved ones.

When I came to the small cottage that was my own, I dismounted and tethered my steed. It was pitch-black beyond the doorway which was wide open. Drawing my sword for safe measure, I warily entered my home.

Rays of silver moonlight shone through the window panes, and I could see that the place was in a state of disorder. The wooden furniture I had constructed was turned over and household items were scattered about on the floor. I was startled by a fleeing pigeon, which fluttered past me and out the door as I disturbed its slumber on my mantle.

I soon sensed another movement.

"Adaira?" I called my wife's name once. There was no answer.

I took a candelabrum from a table and reached for a flint from my pack.

Suddenly, I was struck by a massive blow and knocked to the ground. A familiar sound of screeching and hissing assailed my ears. It was another one of those things! In the darkness I struggled beneath its weight as powerful, clawing hands thrashed at my face. I felt hot, acrid breath on my neck and saw a gleam of white fangs. As it lunged back for attack, I quickly reached up and blocked the jolting bite, catching my steel gauntlet between its jaws instead of letting it rip into my jugular. Then with all my might, I wrenched my arm free of its gnawing grasp and threw the flailing creature from me.

After arising, I stood ready for the lunge I knew it would make. My eyes had adjusted just well enough to see its form, flying at me with killing speed. With a swing of my sword, I severed the head, leaving it lifeless, just as I had the wraith in the cemetery.

Before the blood could even wet the floor, another attack launched upon me, this time from behind. A second creature was now upon my back, its legs wrapped around my torso and deadly jaws lashing down toward my neck. I didn't give this one the chance to get me on the ground. With my free arm, I grabbed the monster by the head and forcefully pulled it off me, slamming it down to the ground and immediately plunging my sword down into where I believed its heart to be. Shrieking once and vomiting forth blood, it lay still, dead at last.

Gasping for breath, I stood in darkness wary for another attack. After a moment, I gradually stumbled to where I dropped the candelabrum and flint upon the floor. Reaching into my pocket with shaking hands, I produced a match from my pocket and lit the three wicks.

What I beheld then when that accursed light illuminated the room struck my heart with an ineffable horror I cannot fully describe—upon the wooden floor before me, in pools of blood lay the dead bodies of my wife and child, as I now realized that it was they who assailed me as undead things in the darkness.

Sorrow and grief overtook me. I fell to the floor and wailed, sobbing mightily over the body of my wife, Adaira. Tears fell in endless streams, mixing with the tainted blood of my loved ones, whom I was forced to slay unknowingly. Despair, regret and defeat were all I knew as my whole world crumbled. My soul burned in mortal agony and I wept long upon the ground, holding and caressing their lifeless bodies in pathetic longing.

As my mind raced, flooding with memories and sadness, despair soon faded and was replaced by a violent rage. I stood and roared at the top of my lungs.

Storming across the room, I came to a large, heavy locked chest I kept near my now broken bedside. Taking the key from my satchel, I opened the box, reached inside and retrieved from it a large, spade-shaped shield of decorated bronze and shining steel. This was adorned with my family crest and was wielded by my forefathers in historical battles of old. Also from the chest I took my father's broadsword which I had kept stowed away and untouched for many years. Armed with these weapons and nothing else, I exited the house, slamming the door in rage, without taking a last glance at my slain family.

That night with malice in my heart and a thousand curses upon my lips, I took torches and set fire to the cottage. There my lady and I had shared the best years of our lives together, and now I stood alone with nothing but memories and rage.

Flames blazed before my eyes and gleamed off the metal sheath of my father's sword. As I stood and watched the house burn, a great hatred seethed through my veins. It was then that I vowed to destroy this race of undead devils and made an oath to myself that Lord Ghormanteia—he who had caused me so much pain—would die slowly by this ancient blade I held.

Once the house had fully burned to the ground I mounted Wrathmane and left the damned town, leaving the place to the night vultures.

* * *

The howling of timber wolves filled the air of the eerie forest. I was now heading back down the dreaded path which had brought me to that house of horror. I rode somberly with the shield of my heritage strapped upon my back and sword at my side.

As I approached, D'vartha the witch was once again outside her hut, crouching near a flaming, bronze brazier which illuminated the area in a ruddy glow. Her garden was now ablaze with iridescence as the weird plants flowed in the air like tentacles. She regarded my coming with a sinister smile upon her face as I dismounted.

"So, you have returned already, dear Karnov," D'vartha said in a mocking tone as she stood facing me with her hands upon her hips.

"I have, witch," I replied.

"And what of your beloved family you were so eager to return to?"

"Slain!" I roared in anger. "Slain by the fangs of those wretched monstrosities! I now vow revenge against this Lord Ghormanteia. I will not rest until he and his kind have perished by the sword of my forefathers, engraving my vengeance upon the blade in blood!"

"I see…" said D'vartha, folding her arms, her bright eyes wide and hair redder than ever in the firelight. "And to what lengths are you willing to go in order to achieve this?"

"I will do whatever is necessary," I said grimly.

The woman smiled mischievously and laughed, clapping her hands once.

"Well then, shall we begin?"

"What are you proposing?" I asked.

"I can grant you an arcane power which will be necessary to battle the vampyre. It will require you to leave your past life behind and sacrifice all that you are. The power will be yours always once I am through."

"I have nothing more to live for now besides fulfilling this task. I'm willing to endure anything."

"All right, then let's get started. Come."

D'vartha walked over to the garth and I followed her. The small, incandescent plants seemed to reach toward me as I came near. They appeared to be throbbing and emitted a hissing, groaning sound.

"These are not ordinary plants," she said.

"I can see that…"

The witch revealed to me a long, pointed dagger held in her right hand. She had rolled up the sleeve of her soiled dress, displaying the fairness of her slender arm. Placing the dagger upon her small wrist, she cut an incision, opening her veins.

At the sight of blood, the mutant vegetation began groaning and lunging toward the open wound. D'vartha held her bleeding wrist above the single largest of the plants, which had a kind of pod above its shrubbery that resembled a head. Down upon it she let the crimson ichor flow. As the blood dripped onto the writhing thing, its pod began to open, revealing sharp thorns in lieu of teeth. D'vartha's lifeblood streamed into the "mouth" and it drank it greedily. The witch took her hand away, and when the herbaceous wretch had devoured all it was given, its vermicular movements ceased, and it remained still for a moment. Using the dagger, she cut a shred of cloth from her frock and quickly bandaged her bleeding wrist.

In an instant I felt the ground where we were standing begin to swell as large roots shot from the plant out into the earth. The verdure convulsed, then began to grow and metamorphose rapidly before our eyes.

As it continued to evolve and expand, new extremities protracted from it that held the likeness of a humanoid. The alchemized foliage shot up until it stood as tall as myself. It was now transmogrified. Bearing a torso of vine, wood, leaves and shrubbery, its legs comprised of the same material were rooted deeply into the earth. In lieu of arms were flailing tentacles with bristles and barbs along their length. The head-like pod was now large and horrible. Its jaws were lined with sharp teeth like razors, and inside was a pink, snaky, worm-like tongue dripping with green liquid. On each side of it were blankly staring eyes like those of a blind reptile, and thick, curving thorns jutted out from its top like devil horns.

I stepped back and drew my sword at the sight of this. D'vartha put her hand upon my shoulder, steadying me. She then spoke to the monster.

"Dark entity of inner earth, your aid has been summoned."

"Why should I aid thee, witch?" replied the monster in a deep, growling tone. "You who have shown no love for our kind, always nourishing us with the foul elemental substance you call water, when all that we desire is earth and fresh blood! I'd rather you come closer so I can devour your flesh!" The creature hissed and licked the air towards her with its serpentine tongue, drooling green saliva all about.

D'vartha reached down, and picked up a nearby pail of water. Lunging forward, she splashed its contents upon the abominable flora, which writhed and shrieked in agony the moment it came in contact with the liquid. Its leafy extensions tensed and quivered.

"Oh, you cruel bitch!" it groaned. "Ask what you will. State your business and be done with me so I can return to my normal state. This wretched form is painful!"

"Reveal to me dark knowledge from beyond the stars. Speak to me the secrets of the Cosmic Ice!" said D'vartha.

"This knowledge you seek is not for those of your kind. It would be dangerous to meddle with such things."

Once again D'vartha threw water upon the monstrous plant. Once again it shuddered and howled.

"Whore of foul enchantments!" it moaned. "Very well—the secret lies in blood… In order to enter the cosmic portals, it must be drunk from the vessels of three soul types; the Living, the Undead and the Earthly Demonic… then power must be summoned from the dark forces of three separate multiversal planes while the proper signs are present…

"But you must beware. There are consequences that…"

Its sentence was cut short, as D'vartha leaped and swung the long dagger, severing the head from it. It toppled to the ground and green ichor sprayed out. The witch brought out a large glass flask from her satchel, uncorked it and grabbed the plant by its giant stem. She then pulled it forward and down, so that from the stump its sustenance poured down into the container. Quickly after this the decapitated horror's limbs wilted, its mutated bulk withered and diminished, shriveling earthward until having the appearance of no more than a dead weed amongst the magically animated botanicals.

"Beware of what?" I asked. "Why didn't you let him finish?"

"Never mind," replied D'vartha as she put the bottle in her sack and wiped the lingering viridity from her blade. "I am now aware of exactly what must be done."

I thought about slapping her for being a dumb bitch but decided not to.

"You said you would be willing to take any measures necessary to achieve your revenge," she said. "So we shall..."

She regarded me with a wry smirk, narrowing her emerald eyes that gleamed in the firelight. I returned her gaze but said nothing.

"I have just collected the blood of the Earthly Demonic," she said. "We must now seek out and acquire that of the Undead. Did you not slay one of them in the cemetery earlier?"

I continued looking at her but remained silent, wondering how she could know of this.

"I thought so." She grinned again. "Let us go."

Chapter III
Summoning the Powers (Phantom Gateways Beckon)

Dense fog surrounded us like soul-hungry ghosts in a haunted monastery when D'vartha and I approached the graveyard double-mounted upon Wrathmane's back. The shale tombstones were brightened by the light of the full moon, and the place appeared to be desolate except for the headless corpse of poor Yashanalla, whom I had slain hours earlier.

Once we dismounted, D'vartha walked over to the body. She set her satchel on the ground and knelt down to put her hand upon the flesh of the dead vampyress.

"The blood will still be good," she said.

From the bag she took her long dagger as well as the decanter containing the demonic plant's life-fluid. She held forth the arm of the girl and cut a large incision, draining a dark crimson flow into the glass container. Once a good amount had been collected, she released the corpse. It was then that she unbandaged her own wrist and squeezed a small amount of blood from the previously opened wound into the vessel to mix with the rest. Once the three blood types were combined, the liquid turned black and an eerie, red vapor began rising from the opening. She sealed it with a cork.

The witch became even paler than usual. Fearing that she might faint from loss of blood, and spill the contents of the container, I knelt down and helped her rise to her feet.

"Will you be all right?" I asked.

"I'll be fine," she said. "We must now begin the ritual. Come."

The crude graves made by the townsfolk were assembled haphazardly in their rows. D'vartha led me over to a crossroads between three tombstones. From her sack she retrieved a black chalk made of bone meal and ash. With this she drew a circle on the hard dirt road, and within it, inscribed symbols of a kind I'd never encountered.

"Move into the circle," she said.

I cautiously did as she instructed, urging Wrathmane into the ring. The witch handed me the carafe of black, curiously-moving liquid. She then stripped herself of clothing, revealing her fair nakedness, gleaming silver in the waxing moonlight.

Afterwards, she took from her stash a struggling black rooster which was bound by the legs, its wings clipped. She held the animal upside down. Waving her long dagger, she made unusual gestures in the air, to the north, south, east and west, and then decapitated the helpless bird. Cock-blood sprayed out. Gathering some of it with her hand, she then began painting symbols upon her nude body with it. These looked similar to the markings she made inside the circle where I stood, but were not exactly the same. After she was finished adorning herself with many of these images, the witch discarded the dead fowl, raised her arms to the heavens and said loudly:

"Dark Lords of the Chaos Spheres, I summon thee. Behold our ceremony of blood and magic. From your fiery thrones, grant us the power we desire…

"I cry to Voraxia, immortal banisher of Ereyth and conceiver of the Eternal Winter, Xarraph, resurrected queen of Ævänah's Chaos realm. I praise Majigormis, Sernam Modan and all the horrors of the Shadowgate. By the green hellfire vomited forth from the severed head of Narjukl, heed my call!

"I ask of Thorn the Godslayer, his demonic sister, Yr, Fenris, father of wolves, and the Shadow Powers of the Elder Dark—Thasaidon, ruler of Zothique's seven hells, the Old Ones and the Worms of the Earth… Come forth and grant us the dark knowledge we seek!

"Lastly, I summon the aid of Zyrashana, witch-queen of Mytos K'unn and Lord Angsaar, the Dark Liege of Chaos. I call upon the powers of the Obsidian Crown and the ancient guardians of the Ice-Veiled Throne of Ultima Thule! May your spirits join ours this night!

"Now Karnov, drink the blood..."

As I uncorked the crystalline jorum, a thick cloud of scarlet fumes rose from it and the dark brew within churned as if alive. I put the opening to my mouth and drank deep. Cringing and shuddering as the fluent substance coated my throat, I swallowed all of it and then threw the flask to the ground in disgust, shattering it.

"What now?" I roared in anger.

Before I could wipe the stuff from my lips, great winds began roaring and the sky appeared to split open above us, revealing a flashing red ether with torrents of blue lightning eddying through it. My horse could stand its ground, but the winds were so powerful that D'vartha was knocked down. She arose to her knees and laughed in triumphant glee, crying aloud with fists held to the sky.

"Yes! Great Lords empower us!" bellowed the witch.

D'vartha looked more insane than ever, unclad and painted in the carmine skylight, her long hair blowing wildly in the wind and green eyes blazing with an indescribable madness.

There was a massive blast as a huge bolt of lightning struck before me in the circle, blinding me and causing the earth to tremble. When my vision cleared, I realized that upon the ground, the symbols now radiated with a pulsing blue light.

"By the Gods!" exclaimed D'vartha, struggling to stay afoot in the raging winds.

I looked dazedly into the hypnotic, swirling markings that entranced me as I gazed. Carefully, I took a step back, staying within the circumference of the ring.

"Brace yourself, Karnov!" shouted the witch.

I looked at her with a questioning expression, not understanding.

At that very moment, a second boom sounded, as another bolt of lightning cracked the sky and came down upon me and my steed. My body convulsed wildly and I was engulfed in a seething mass of galvanic current. The levin did not cease when it struck, but continued to surge from the ether into me. As the energy flowed through my bones, I felt a sensation colder than the highest snow wyrm-infested mountains and an intense, tingling pain run throughout my being. My blood felt as if it was freezing in my veins and my mind reeled in a terrible insanity. Wrathmane and I levitated, immersed in the lightning orb.

On her knees, D'vartha beheld this with a deranged beam of exuberance upon her face, laughing with victorious pride.

"Yes! Hold on, Karnov!"

As the shock continued, I felt a change come over me, and a swelling transformation occurred. Something was overtaking my body and limbs. A hard, ice-like substance started to encase me. The sensation of intense pain and confusion that had assailed me now changed into an exhilaration of overwhelming joy and ecstasy. The hard, icy matter encasing me materialized into an armor of frozen blue steel. It covered my whole frame. A helm of the same material also developed upon my head. Engraved in the armor were blue-glowing symbols identical to the arcane runes D'vartha had illustrated within the occultic annulus.

Ghostly forms arose, issuing from the glyphs. They appeared to be grotesque phantoms of the undead—transparent beings that moaned eerily, with hollow eyes and fangs protruding from their mouths. These ghosts rose from the earth and flew into me, being absorbed by the lucent sigils in my armor that coincided with those from which they came forth. After a wraith from each symbol was assimilated into me, the stream of sorcerous lightning overtaking my body ceased and the winds died so that all was still.

D'vartha stared wide-eyed at my new form in silence. I sat upon my mount, inside the illumined wreath. A ghostly aura now flowed all along my icy mail, undulating inside it as if part of the armor. The phantom-energy embraced me and I could see the hideous faces of the undead entities in it. I realized that the sword in my grasp and the shield upon my back cast an azurean luster and had the same spiritual substance flowing throughout.

It was not only I that had been changed; Wrathmane was now garbed as a noble warhorse in the same rune-inscribed ghost-armor, his eyes flaring with an ultramarine radiance. I stretched my limbs and gripped the hilt of my enchanted weapon, feeling stronger and mightier than ever, my mind clear and sharp and somehow enlightened…

D'vartha rose to her feet, still staring at me in awe. Her smile faded.

"Now, dismount and come forth so that I can reveal to you the secrets of the Cosmic Ice."

I acknowledged the witch with a glance from beneath my helm of icy steel and spirit-fleece. I did as she asked and stepped out of the ring towards her. The sounds of night-creatures had ceased and only the cool breeze whispered as I stood before her like an otherworldly knight.

"Listen carefully," she said. "By the powers of blood and divine sorcery, you have now been transformed into a phantom-clad warrior and voyager of the Cosmic Ice, which is a gateway to a series of passageways that lead to various places on this earthly plane and beyond. When you slay an undead being, the tainted soul of the creature will be absorbed into your magic armor. Not only will you gain strength and power by imbibing their essence, but your armor and weapons will become 'charged.' When that occurs, you will be granted the ability to open the gateways. At no other time will this be possible.

"As you know, the deadly mountain range which Ghormanteia's castle sits upon is unscalable. No man, even you in your new form, could pass through the force field which has been placed upon them. Now that you are energized with undead souls, you can travel through the Cosmic Ice beyond the force field, directly to the great fortress. I will show you how to open the gateway.

"The runes upon your armor represent different planar gateways which you may journey through. When you draw one of these symbols upon the ground with your weapon, a portal will open and you may traverse the plane that coincides with the sigil you have drawn. Again, this will only work when your sword and armor are 'charged' by souls of the vampyres you have slain. Each passage leads to a different place in this world, which you can reach by utilizing them. Some of these pathways guide to worlds beyond, as well. You will soon become familiar with the symbols and the roads which each are connected to."

D'vartha came forward and touched one of the many pulsating runes upon my breastplate—the one that looked like a chalice with a crescent moon behind it.

"This is the sign to open the specific gateway that will take you beyond the deadly mountains and directly to Ghormanteia's castle. Now, with the point of your sword, draw it upon the ground."

I grasped the great brand of my ancestors which now seemed to radiate with life. Putting the point of the blade to the earth, I did as she instructed. This happened with ease, and my hand moved automatically, as if it were an extension of the weapon. The intricate marking was etched so quickly that it was as if I had thoroughly perfected the skill many years ago. The crest gave off an uncanny flare just like the ones upon my armor.

Once completed, the insignia I had made brightened and great beams of bluish light shot up to the sky. It wavered and materialized into a pool of icy luminosity that swirled with myriad prismatic colors, illuminating the whole scene.

"You've done it!" D'vartha exclaimed, shielding her eyes from the blinding light. "Go forward, Karnov. You now have the power to conquer the Undead Lord. Heed my words and be victorious. Claim your vengeance and cleanse these lands!"

I looked down into the shimmering portal. Memories of my fallen wife and son ran through my mind, clear as ever and I scowled.

"These lands, ha!" I said. "All I care for these lands is drenching them in the blood of Ghormanteia and his kind. It is only vengeance I am concerned with, and that I shall have! Thank you witch, and farewell… No doubt, we shall meet again."

D'vartha stared at me with tears welling in her crystalline jade eyes. Fearless and ready, I mounted Wrathmane. Taking one last look at the trembling witch, I urged Wrathmane into the portal… and the Age of Karnov had begun.

Book II
by Howie K. Bentley

Chapter I
Into the Lair of the Fiend

Sparks flew from Wrathmane's hooves as we galloped along the swirling hollow of Cosmic Ice, traversing the boundaries of space and time. Ahead of me lay the lair of the vampyre, Lord Ghormanteia—he who would perish by my sword before the sun rose on the decimated village I once called home. The phantom wisps lingering about my armor melded with the mystical blue ice and coruscated into whirling colors and faces of heroes who had travelled the Cosmic Ice in ages long fallen to dust—as well as those who would travel this road in the far-flung future. They whispered their exhortations and urged me onward.

Scenes born of the Cosmic Ice and the ensorcelled armor that I wore surrounded me. All around raged the battle between spear-wielding warriors from the dawn of man, engaged in bloody conflict with serpent-men. The primitives drove their spears into the reptilians, and green ichor sprayed over the cave dwellers' furs and powerful naked limbs. The scene dissolved into mist and reformed anew as armored vampyre warriors stormed a castle and were beaten back by a single warrior clad in glowing runic armor much like my own. The vampyre hordes fell before the lone champion's battle-axe like chaff before the scythe.

The castle of the axe-wielding warrior receded into the mists of time to be replaced by boar-headed brutes roasting a little girl on a spit. The child looked to be about eight years old. The hog-men turned the screaming child round and round over a fire while more of the villains held her family members still and made them watch. A gallant knight in phantom-haunted armor raced in on his horse, and the hog-men fell before his whirling blade. The armored avenger did not stop until he ran the last brute down and split his head open with his sword. Crimson gushed, and bits of bone and pieces of brain scattered. The knight raised his blood-soaked steel in triumph; then, he looked at me and nodded. I felt a kinship with those who had waged the timeless battle against the abominations that would forever plague the sons of man, but I needed nothing but the hatred in my heart to spur my mount further into the lair of the fiend. I kicked my heels into my horse's sides and urged Wrathmane forward. The heroes' faces and scenes of past triumphs waned and faded away as I approached the end of the netherworld ice-tunnel that bore its way through time.

My horse leapt from the exit of the tunnel, and a blinding light exploded. Darkness descended upon me and my mount. My eyes adjusted to the dimly-lit chamber and Wrathmane stood on his hind legs, screaming and kicking his hoofs in the air in response to the abominations before us.

"Greetings, O mighty slayer of the undead!" mocked the abhorrence lolling on his throne in front of me. The vampyre lord's green face was framed by shoulder-length, straight black hair that shined like polished onyx. He seemed undisturbed by my presence as he stared into a crystal orb containing an eldritch object as if he was more interested in what he saw there. His ebony eyes beamed with the insane fevered glow of one who has been infested with daemons for aeons. His face snarled sourly—with an upturned nose like a bat—and was drawn into a perpetual rictus of hatred and cruelty.

"Won't you join in our revelry tonight?" he asked as he put the crystal orb in his pocket and relaxed on his throne, waving his left arm. The billowing sleeve of his purple silk robe seemed to multiply and trail itself when he moved his arm. Long claw-like talons protruded from the end of his sleeve and indicated the pleasures that he referred to as he swept his arm: naked women, horned like rams and both alabaster and scarlet in color, writhed on the floor with one another in the throes of Sapphic ecstasy.

A newly-turned vampyress sat at the foot of Ghormanteia's throne, clutching her knees to her chest and rocking back and forth in anguish. About her neck was a thick iron collar, and fastened to it was a length of heavy chain links that wrapped around the arm of the vampyre lord's ornate crystal throne.

A young girl brought in a wailing infant. Upon first sight, I judged that the girl carrying the child couldn't have been more than ten years of age, but I knew by the elongated teeth that she bared when she smiled at Ghormanteia's starving fledgling that the girl could have been centuries old. The girl child laid the baby before the starving woman and Ghormanteia's vampyre-slave wept as she sunk her fangs into the screaming infant. The woman's hair covered the baby's face, but I could see blood running down its tiny convulsing body; then I was lost in a barrage of fleeting thoughts. A feeling of intoxication engulfed me, and I nearly fell off my horse. I watched the vampyre lord roar with laughter and all I could think of was, "By the gods of Averoigne! That bastard is ugly!"

As my eyes adjusted more to the gloom, I realized the vastness of the vampyre lord's hall. Off to the right, smoke issued forth from a brazier filling the room with a sickly sweet aroma, redolent of dangerous eldritch flowers—masking a faint hint of charnel-house decay. The smoke permeated the vile sights before me like fog filling up a graveyard.

"How do you like the yellow lotus, Slayer?" Ghormanteia cackled—as if he could read my thoughts. His voice dropped in pitch and sounded as though many men were echoing his words. "It is quite alluring isn't it? My playthings love what the flower brings to my chamber—fortunately, I am immune. I always say such things are good for the slaves, but not for the masters."

I had only been in Ghormanteia's throne room for what seemed like seconds, but the yellow lotus had scattered my thoughts and made me forget momentarily what I had come to do. I looked down upon the floor to see the succubi sensuously rubbing their bodies on a young dead girl and wallowing on her like a dog on carrion. They rolled over and held their outstretched hands up to Ghormanteia, petitioning their evil god to bestow a guerdon upon them.

Ghormanteia reached into a pocket inside his robe and brought forth crystal-clear straws, which had thin hollow blades on the end and were made from some strange, pliable material. The female daemons turned their attention back to the dead girl and drove the bladed straws into various parts of her body. They sucked on the straws, and I could see the blood flowing through the clear tubes into their mouths. They kissed one another and transferred the blood between them—swapping it back and forth before swallowing it—while licking and caressing each other. Though my head still swam in a narcotic haze, I whipped my broadsword from its scabbard and pointed it at Ghormanteia. Wrathmane was obviously stunned by the effects of the yellow lotus as well as I. He merely let out a disinterested neigh as I pointed my sword at the vampyre lord and addressed him. "Ghormanteia, vampyre lord of Thornhaven, formerly of Aschorzotha! This night I condemn you to death by my sword for the murders of my wife and son and those who once dwelt in my village… and other places…"

My rightful accusations of the vampyre lord made him smile: he nodded his head when I condemned him, accepting my challenge.

"You! Vile abomination! A master of the black arts who cannot even be bothered to cast a glamour upon yourself to mask the hideousness of your own countenance!" I shouted.

Ghormanteia's sinister grin faded and he leaned forward on his throne like a jungle cat ready to spring, hissing at me and spewing forth bloody spittle from his fanged mouth as he pressed a button on the arm of his chair—his throne disappearing through a trapdoor in the floor. Scant seconds had passed when Ghormanteia's throne reemerged without the vampyre lord. In Ghormanteia's place, a giant white serpent entwined his throne. The serpent's alabaster skin glistened and its forked tongue flickered as fast as lightning—its open mouth revealing deadly hook-like fangs.

"Vampyre slayer, meet White Wyrm!" I could hear Ghormanteia's reverberating cachinnations, but I could not see him.

"Coward!" I cried out.

More of the vampyre's echoing laughter bounced around the chamber. I moved my horse from side to side, looking for the fiend, but he made no appearance.

Wrathmane backed up—rearing and screaming—trying to turn away from the serpent. My mighty steed wanted no part of the giant snake, and, in truth, with the state I was in from inhaling the fumes of the yellow lotus, neither did I; but I thought of my dead loved ones and rage surged through me like burning lava, filling my veins! I dug my booted heels into Wrathmane's ribs and swore. My mount leapt forward, and I swung my sword at the head of White Wyrm. The colossal serpent quickly ducked its head and struck back at me. I leaned back in my saddle just in time to avoid the deadly hook-like fangs and thrust upward with my sword. The snake dropped its head to one side, avoiding my blade, and dived onto the floor, leaving Ghormanteia's throne vacant. In a flash, White Wyrm had coiled about me and Wrathmane, breathing its venomous fetor upon us. The serpent's coils squeezed me and my mount, robbing us of the opportunity of any movement. My sword arm was tightly pinned to my side. The giant snake threw its head back in triumph, and venom sprayed from his fangs and rained down upon me; but I felt no pain. Losing consciousness and floating outside of myself, I watched as Wrathmane and I became a shimmering gaseous substance that faded into the ether and vanished from Castle Thornhaven.

Chapter II
Exiled

The frantic pounding of Wrathmane's hooves was the first thing I remember once my scrambled brain had reassembled itself. The horse galloped as if we were being chased by the Hounds of Tindalos. After much effort I brought my mount to a stop and surveyed my surroundings. A dim purple sun in the eastern sky cast a soothing violet hue over the landscape in which I found myself. Low rocky hills spread out across the horizon occasionally marked by jutting stratum appearing at random intervals. The ground was completely flat and even, devoid of any vegetation. Everything that lay under the sky of this strange land matched the color of the dim violet rays radiating from its sun. The air was neither too hot, nor too cold.

I spurred my mount on and rode for some time, expecting the tranquil violet landscape to change at some point, and hoping to meet a denizen of this weird world. Memories of my encounter with the vampyre lord's giant pet snake back at Castle Thornhaven returned to me, and though I knew not where I was or how I had arrived here, I was glad that I yet lived another day to exact my vengeance on the slayer of my wife and son. The glowing runes upon my armor had long extinguished. I now needed to seek one who would inform me of the ways of this new world and direct me to a local nest of vampyres, so that I could plunge my steel into their wicked hearts and charge my armor with their vile blood, opening the gates to again traverse the Cosmic Ice back to Ghormanteia's lair.

My mouth was dry, and I longed to quench my thirst. We had travelled for what seemed like hours in this barren violaceous land when Wrathmane came to an abrupt stop, slightly tilted his head back and sniffed the air. A feeling of elation and relief spread over me, as I knew the horse smelled water nearby. I knew that he was thirsty too after all that we had been through with the vampyre, the giant snake, and our intoxication from the yellow lotus. Cool, clear water was at that moment more valuable than gold to me. I loosened my hold on the horse's bridle and let him take us to water.

* * *

Having quenched my thirst and tethered my mount to a thin layer of rock jutting up from the ground, I filled my two canteens, replaced them in my saddlebag, lay down on the ground, close to the waterhole but out of sight, and fell asleep.

I don't know how long I had lain in slumber when a woman's scream brought me awake. I was quickly on my feet with sword drawn, but I could see no one. This was good: at least I had the element of surprise in my favor if the situation was as bad as it sounded.

I heard the woman scream again, this time followed by the laughter and speech of men. I could not hear the words they said to the woman, but by the tone of their speech, I sensed mockery. The voices emanated from over the hill before me, and off to my right.

Stealthily, I moved as a phantom in the night and untethered Wrathmane from the stratum where I had left him. I patted my horse on his side and gently took his bridle and led him up the hill. When we reached the hill's summit, I saw the men. I quickly pulled my mount down to the ground and ducked my head behind a large rock where I could watch what occurred below.

Five men accosted a slim yellow-haired woman. All five of them were armed with swords and daggers. The rogues were clad in leather armor, loose-fitting breeches, knee-high soft leather boots, and shirts of coarse material, but for one, who went about bare-chested. The men slung her around like a rag-doll and shoved her back and forth to one another. She screamed, "I would rather die than to be sold into slavery and used as a whore by the vermin of Klahr-Atoch!"

The man who now had a hold of her was a thin wiry rogue with a moustache. His face resembled that of a rat. "Well, you just relax, girl. We'll get you trained right now in the profession of whoring, so you'll be ready when we reach the city," the rat-faced man jeered.

The others burst out laughing at Rat-Face's jest as the woman spun around and tried to hit him, but the man caught her by both of her wrists and wagged his tongue at her. She struggled to free her hands from his grasp and spit in his face. The rat-faced man slapped her hard, and she fell to the ground, sobbing. A tall silent man had been standing by watching stoically. The expression on his face never changed. He nodded to a giant with a shaved head and a ring in each ear.

The large man wasn't wearing a shirt. The stoic man was obviously their leader. He spoke with a drawl and told the woman sternly, "Oortok here is going to see to it that you are ready for anything that they tell you to do once you come off that auction block, girl."

The big man unfastened his belt and walked toward the woman who was sobbing and crawling across the ground. He folded his belt over twice and chortled, his grin taking up most of his face.

The stoic man calmly told the oversized simpleton, "That's it, Oortok. Let her know beforehand what happens when she doesn't cooperate. It will make it easier to train her."

Rat-Face and another of the slavers held the woman while Oortok stood in front of her grinning, his pants lying on the ground. No sooner had Rat-Face ripped the top of her dress open, revealing her small perky breasts, than I was riding down upon them, the element of surprise to my advantage. Wrathmane charged in among the men. Oortok had almost pulled his pants up when my cold steel met his manhood and left it shorn upon the dirt. The big man screamed and blood jettisoned from his groin. He fell, kneeling with his head on the ground. I slashed another slaver's throat as I rode through the space where they were gathered, and turned to face the remaining three vermin.

All three men were brandishing steel. The leader of the slavers whipped out his dagger and threw it. He aimed for my right eye, but I ducked my head to one side and felt the wind off of the weapon as it went whistling by. I retaliated with a dagger thrown to my assailant's throat. The stoic leader lay on the ground clutching at the handle of my weapon, gurgling and bleeding out onto the violaceous surface of this strange world. That was the first and last time his countenance had shown any emotion since I had met him. His face now wore an eternal mask of pain.

Rat-Face shoved his fellow slaver to the side and ran in, aiming his sword stroke at Wrathmane's legs; but my warhorse reared on his hind legs and the man's blade sliced through empty air. Wrathmane brought his legs back down, and I split my attacker's head open. Shards of bone and bits of brain splattered and went flying—his dead body folding as it fell. The remaining slaver ran for his life, but I kicked my heels into Wrathmane's sides and he gave chase. With one blow of my broadsword, I cut the man down as he ran. The blade sliced through his collar bone and sank into his torso. He let out a grunt as he fell.

I turned my steed and rode back to see how the young woman was faring. She clutched at her torn dress to cover her bosom, and sobbed, averting her eyes in shame and fear of what I might do, now that I was alone with her.

"What is your name, woman?" I inquired.

She continued to clutch at herself and weep.

"They won't be able to harm you anymore. They will not rise again," I said.

I climbed down from my saddle and held out my hand. She looked at me and then down at the ground. I moved my hand, offering it to her again. She looked up at me, and her hand embraced mine.

"There are more of them," she softly spoke.

"How many?"

"Maybe twenty," she answered.

"Then let us be away!" I replied. "In which direction do they travel?"

She pointed south. I had been travelling west, so I guided Wrathmane west and told the woman, "We will distance ourselves from them, for now."

We walked over to my horse, and I jumped back into the saddle. Reaching down, I scooped her up with one arm and tossed her behind me.

"Hold on tightly," I said.

I heard her exhale nervously, "What is your name, warrior?" She cried out in a shaking voice over the pounding of Wrathmane's thundering hooves.

"I am Karnov! By what name are you called woman?" I shouted in response.

"I am Qoulitiax!" she called out in reply—her voice sounding steadier than before.

Chapter III
Qoulitiax

Darkness had fallen, and the weird world in which I had found myself had changed in color from a violet day to a dim blue nighttime. The land was faintly lit by a glowing sapphire moon, high in the sky. The place was barren and devoid of vegetation, but Qoulitiax had gathered a type of flammable rocks that had easily ignited when rubbed together; we now sat before a fire that staved off the chill of the benighted azure desert.

We ate in silence, satisfying our hunger on the remainder of some dried meat and fruit that I had taken from my saddlebag.

Washing down the remainder of my meal with a long drink from my canteen, I passed the water to Qoulitiax; she drank what was left. I had one more canteen of water to last us until we made it out of the desert and to a village or city where water was available.

I had sat in silence long enough. I needed answers to form a plan to get back to castle Thornhaven and destroy Lord Ghormanteia. "What is this land called, Qoulitiax?"

"This is Colbalus Violac, the Violet Desert—only... it is blue at night," she replied.

"I see that," I said, "but I wasn't referring to the desert itself, so much as this world in general."

She stared at me, unsure what to say.

"What world is this, where the desert is of a violet hue in the daytime and a glowing blue at night? What do you call the world in which you live?" I prompted her.

She stared at me for a moment as if I were insane. "To the west lie the Braethurian Isles: Vaengland, Laeciffia, Turnia, and Rittenarg. To the north of Braethuria, separated by the Thoorian Sea is Dythland; and to the north of that, the Scaelavian lands of Tyrthunia and Njordgraath. Above them lie only the frozen wastelands."

She paused, her face turning red, expecting me to burst out in laughter at any moment. When I did not laugh, she continued, "Across the Thurian Sea and far inland begins the Colbalus Violac desert—where we are now. It must be crossed to reach Asstyria to the south and the Vingilian city of unlimited pleasures, Klahr-Atoch. That is where the caravan of slavers from which you helped me escape is bound. Eastward lies the Chang-Liam empires bordered on each side by the Dong-Hite and Tung-Hite Seas."

I sat quietly, mulling over all that the girl had told me until she interrupted the silence. "Were you injured in the fight with the slavers? You moved so quickly; I did not see any of the men who were even able to strike a blow at you. Did you suffer an injury to your head that affects your memory?"

"Nay, woman." I thought it futile to try to explain my situation. For a moment I sat in silence, taking in the features of my new-found companion. Her blues eyes shone high above prominent cheekbones. Her nose was mildly aquiline and her wavy blonde hair spilled over her shoulders, reaching far down her back. For the first time, I noticed how much her beauty shined through all of the dirt and hardship etched on her face.

By now Qoulitiax had come to the realization that I was not going to harm her, and she began to relate her tale to me.

"I am the daughter of Count Magne of Turnia. I was kidnapped by the Njordgraathians in a raid on the coast of Vaengland while I was there visiting my sister, Nincia, who is married to Prince Haardvolg. Out of fear of the hatred that the Njordgraathians have for my people, most of all those who occupy the Braethurian Isles, I dared not reveal my identity. I was sold to slavers who put in at a neutral port below Dythland. There were nearly two hundred of us locked in cages and transported across this desert to be sold on the auction blocks in Klahr-Atoch. We were fed and watered like animals. None of the men had molested me, but they had done some terrible things to some of the other girls. There was a man back there you killed. You split his head open with your sword."

"The rat-faced man?" I asked.

"Yes. His face resembled that of a rat. He had been watching me for days. I knew he was going to try to outrage me. The cage had been opened for feeding time and hadn't been properly latched back. I saw my opportunity and took it. It was hopeless, but I would rather have died than be used like some of the other unfortunates who were locked away with me had been."

I nodded my head in agreement with her.

"Even worse was what awaited me had I made it to Klahr-Atoch," she added. "The rough-handed soldiers and cruel fat merchants of the city are the mildest of the fates that can befall one such as myself there." She shuddered.

"How is this?" I asked her.

"Xycanthia! Her reputation is known all the way back in my homeland in Turnia. She is fond of young girls and the horrors and experiments she carries out on them are legendary. She is a vampyre!"

"Where is this vampyress? I must plunge my sword into her wicked heart as soon as possible, so that I may return by the Cosmic Ice to Castle Thornhaven and destroy Lord Ghormanteia, the murderer of my family!" The mention of this vampyre, Xycanthia, had been like cold water thrown into my face.

I looked up at the azure moon casting its rays over this blue nighttime land and took a deep breath.

"Listen, woman," I said, and I related my tale of woe to her.

* * *

". . . And that is how I was exiled to this world by the vampyre, Lord Ghormanteia, and his giant pet snake, White Wyrm; and I seek the means to return to my world and strike his grotesque head from his body. I must have the blood of the vamypress to perform the ritual to go back to my world and

Castle Thornhaven wherein resides he whom I must destroy."

Qoulitiax nodded her head and without hesitating she said, "I will go with you!"

I held up my hand and told her, "Such a mission is much more dangerous than dealing with common slavers, woman. You have no experience of these supernatural creatures and their ways."

"I owe you my life for saving me from the slavers."

"You owe me nothing! I am the veteran of many wars, not only with dumb brutes brandishing steel, but creatures that populate a blackened world only experienced in nightmare by most men: vampyres, witches, wizards hurling dark enchantments upon me, and men who rise up from death to walk again and wield weapons once forged for the living. All of these things I have fought! Most of my life has been one long battle against the forces of darkness and the agents of evil!"

"So, how are you to get into Xycanthia's abode?" Qoulitiax asked. "Do you have a plan?"

"Well, it certainly won't be to burst into her chamber, waving my sword this time," I mumbled, after a long pause.

I held my head in my hand and rubbed my face.

Qoulitiax cocked her head to one side and looked up into my face as I raised my head.

"I know that you are not fey from a head-wound sustained in battle, and I believe your story to be true. I have also heard of Xycanthia's evil and it threatens all women… and men in the world that I know. You do not know this world. You are a stranger here, exiled by the vampyre lord. But I have travelled in the south before."

I sat silently listening to Qoulitiax's argument for her coming along.

* * *

"And do you not agree that a woman's weapon is cunning? It is instilled in us by nature!" she said excitedly.

I nodded my head in agreement.

"So it is settled!" She clapped her hands and added gleefully, "Now, I have a plan. Listen!"

Chapter IV
Xycanthia

Once we had crossed the Violet Desert, and reached the city, the landscape appeared much like that of any of the other southern lands in which I have travelled. The sun no longer shone violet, and it looked like the one that cast its rays upon the world that I knew. I purchased a chestnut mare for Qoulitiax from a merchant back in the city state of Asstyria. Gold coin was the preferred monetary unit, no matter what weird world one found himself in. We had ridden long before reaching Klahr-Atoch and refreshed ourselves on food and drink as we made our way through the milling throngs of the bazaar in search of one who might sell me information as to the whereabouts of Xycanthia's abode. Gold coinage again did not fail me and it wasn't long before we were riding for the village of Cachtice, on the outskirts of Klahr-Atoch.

The owner at the Dragon's Bane Inn made it perfectly clear that he did not want our staying there that night, but my sword point at his throat changed his mind; and we slept there. I needed a good night's sleep before dealing with any more vampyres. At the mention of Xycanthia's name, the entire inn had fallen silent, as they usually do in these situations. But for a few gold coins, a desperate barmaid, who engaged me in clandestine conversation, led me to a stable boy who was willing to sell us information as to how to find Xycanthia, and lead us to her domain.

Dusk had set in when we arrived at the winding road leading up to Xycanthia's aerie. Qoulitiax rode alongside of me. I brought Wrathmane to a stop and Qoulitiax reined in beside me with her mare. The black citadel stood in the center, ringed by walls and towers. A full moon rose over the massive barbican supported by flying buttresses on either side. A winged creature circled high above the top of the edifice, and dipped down to the raised battlements of the castle before ascending again. I had seen the vampyre in its many forms and presumed this to be Xycanthia. She knew she had guests.

Darkness fully enveloped the castle as we reached the summit on which rested Xycanthia's lair. As we led our mounts in front of the castle, torches in sconces—which were lined along the walls of the castle—burst into flame.

"The stable boys will see to your mounts," came a husky feminine voice from an open window above.

Two short figures in dirty brown hooded robes appeared and took our horses' reins. Qoulitiax drew back in horror at the creatures' sewn together mouths and their white eyes, as though they had rolled them back in their heads. I nodded to Qoulitiax, reassuring her that it would be all right.

A heavy oaken door opened, seemingly of its own volition; and the woman's voice rang out again: "Come on up!"

We ascended the forebuilding steps to Xycanthia's abode, and made our way through the gatehouse leading into the castle keep.

Though these were just architectural features, there was something sinister that permeated even the carved arches and columns of Xycanthia's keep. The windows were darkened with voluminous drapes and paintings hung at varying intervals on the ancient stone walls of the chamber. One picture showed a young lady's body laid out on a funeral slab, her dead eyes gazing upon oblivion, while a winged woman hovered over her and gently caressed the corpse's milk-white throat with her tongue. A droplet of blood trickled down the dead girl's throat. I couldn't help but notice the resemblance of the demonic woman depicted in the painting to the witch D'vartha, whom I knew from my own world. Another larger painting revealed an orgy wherein humans and demons writhed on the floor, their blood-stained mouths forming into an "O" in convulsing faces, screaming and grunting in ecstasy. One mysterious painting showed cloaked figures gathered around a giant, performing surgery on it. Only one face of the sinister physicians was revealed and it looked straight at me with its mottled countenance as if it truly lived. Its tongue seemed to flicker out of its mouth as I looked upon its grinning reptilian features. I cared not to gaze upon such an abomination and quickly looked away.

"I have been expecting you," came a sultry voice from the top of the stairs. Her long ruby-red hair spilled over shoulders and down her back. She seemed to float down the stairs—instead of walk—in her saturnine evening gown. She turned her burning emerald gaze upon me.

My eyes came to rest on the fairest alabaster face I have ever seen. "D'vartha!" I burst out. She stopped on the spiraling stairwell and cocked her head inquisitively, a look of surprise turning to one of amusement.

"My apologies, fair lady. I momentarily mistook you for another. Though not as lovely as you!" I quickly assured her.

Xycanthia reached the bottom of the stairs and stepped onto the floor of the chamber. As she did so, a hulking brute in a robe such as the "stable boys" had worn, albeit much larger, appeared. His hands were concealed in his sleeves. The thing's head was massive and protruded from its body considerably. Its misshapen head was concealed by the same brown fabric from which its robe was made. All that showed was its filmy blue eyes set wide apart. His eyes constantly shifted as they peered at us through slits cut in the fabric concealing his entire head.

Our host said, "Follow Gruterrig! He will lead you to the feasting hall. You must be famished. I will join you shortly and you can tell me of your travels…" and she added with a hint of menace in her voice, "…and how you ended up here."

* * *

Xycanthia licked her sensuous crimson lips and eyed Qoulitiax seductively as my companion pecked like a bird at the roasted vegetables and bread on her plate. "Eat, child! You have hardly touched your dinner, and I know that you must be starving."

I am suspicious of vampyres—especially one as beautiful as Xycanthia—but the meat that she called beef ribs looked genuine to me; and I was hungry enough that I chose to believe that they didn't come from a human. As I filled up on food and drink I let Qoulitiax continue to answer Xycanthia's questions.

"You say you were kidnapped by Njordgraathian raiders and sold to a slave caravan until Karnov rescued you. How was it that Karnov chanced upon the slavers' caravan?"

"As I told you before, my father is Count Magne of Turnia. He hired the best mercenaries that gold could procure, and Karnov tracked down the slave caravan and rescued me," Qoulitiax explained.

Xycanthia cast her wanton gaze upon me. "Well, he certainly looks dangerous," the vampyress stated, relaxing her posture and licking her lips invitingly.

I pretended not to notice and washed down a mouthful of beef with what I was pretty sure was red wine. A young girl in a billowing white gown flowed into the room and came over to Xycanthia. Her garment was stained in the front with crimson, and I was pretty sure it was not red wine. I was also fairly certain that it was a burial gown that she was wearing. The girl's complexion was wan, and she was entranced. Her flaxen hair was combed back and fell over her shoulders.

"Don't come in here like that! Go get changed before you join us!" Xycanthia snapped at the girl.

The girl said nothing; she just bowed her head and shuffled languorously from the room.

"Whence do you come, Karnov?" asked Xycanthia.

"A place called Dahlradia. It is in the northernmost corner of Laeciffia. Centuries ago, it was known for its diamond mines; but in this age, it has fallen into obscurity; and most have never heard of it."

"I have heard of it," Xycanthia responded haughtily. "I have been there, but that was long ago when the place was still relevant," she said, grinning and showing a glimpse of her fangs in the flickering candlelight for the first time that evening.

"Who lives here with you?" I said, attempting to find out more about her defenses before I swept lovely Xycanthia's head from her shoulders with cold steel.

"There is just myself and a few servants. That is all that I require, other than the company of pretty young ladies like Isle here." She indicated the girl whom she had scolded only moments agone; Xycanthia's tone was now sweet as honey. The girl held her hand out to Xycanthia and the vampyress took it and seated Isle close beside her.

Isle had seen fifteen summers or less, if she had been recently turned, as I suspected.

"Occasionally I like to have a big, strong warrior like yourself. On a special occasion, it is nice to have both," Xycanthia said, licking her lips again.

Why was I plagued with beautiful redheads full of treachery and black witchery?

"The road out of Klahr-Atoch leads straight to Nehbrektahr, the obvious point by which you would ferry to the closest port at Braenaxtra to board a ship for passage back to Turnia. How did you end up in Cachtice?" Xycanthia inquired.

"The merchant at the bazaar in Klahr-Atoch told us that Cachtice lay next to Nehbrektahr, and by taking this route it would shorten our travel to the ferry by half a day," Qoulitiax answered. "I am anxious to return to my family as soon as possible."

"Well the merchant lied," Xycanthia put in angrily, and then, her wicked smile returning, she added with a slight pause "…or…"

The two short creatures with their white eyes and sewn mouths appeared again and shuffled across the floor in their voluminous brown robes to refill our wine cups. Qoulitiax held up her hand and said, "No more for me. I am tired and feel the need to bed down, if you would be so kind, Lady Xycanthia." My companion stood up.

"I had better do the same; we must be on our way at daybreak," I added, rising from my chair. The room filled up with tension, and the last thing I needed was for Qoulitiax to get separated from me.

"Gruterrig!" Xycanthia called. No sooner had she said his name than he appeared close behind me. I could hear his heavy breathing just over my shoulder.

"Show them to their room… in the dungeon!" Xycanthia screamed.

I whipped my broadsword from its scabbard and spun to face Gruterrig. He stepped back and raised his arms, his robe falling away to reveal deadly gleaming steel. Where his forearms and hands should have been, there were, instead, two short wicked swords. His upper arms were masses of muscle and his face was a grotesque mask from which an axe blade protruded beneath his shaved pate. He groaned and grunted through a mouth that had been long sewn together, and his insane blue eyes beamed at me from his withered mummy-like face. The hulking brute's whole body was muscular except for his protruding belly which contained a large singular blue eye that burned with rage; in unison with those in his head.

The monster moved toward me and I swung my sword in a deadly arc that let him know that this was not going to be easy.

"I knew you were no mere mercenary when I saw you at my door. The stench of vampyre hunter was all over you, and that trollop following you around like a lost bitch puppy is the worst liar in the world!" Xycanthia shouted.

The vampyress had her arms at her sides, her palms cupped and turned upward; and she was moving her lower arms up and down in a circular motion. She started transforming into the bat-like creature that I had seen encircling her castle when we had arrived. From a pouch at my belt, I quickly took some powdered vervain mixed with an assortment of other herbs that vampyres dread and flung them into Xycanthia's face.

She changed back to her semi-human form and fell against the wall, choking. As Gruterrig moved forward, I swung my sword at him once again. I then leapt upon the table and back off, landing beside Isle, and with one sword stroke I sent her head rolling upon the dining room table, spilling the contents of what was left of my wine—with a thump and a ding.

"Qoulitiax, get behind me! Stay close!" I growled. Runic shapes appeared before my eyes and I quickly traced them on the floor with my sword-point. I could feel my armor pulsing with the essence of the slain fledgling as it ignited the power of the Cosmic Ice.

Gruterrig's eyes shifted quickly, and for a moment I thought that he might choose to try to escape, but he came charging at me wildly with his axe-laden head thrown back and his arms whirling swords. Like lightning I tore my dagger from its sheath and hurled it into the monster's giant eye glaring out from its belly. The sickly sky-blue eye jetted crimson and Gruterrig doubled up with a horrible groan and fell on the floor. I wasted no time, springing to where he had fallen. I chopped his head off with my sword; it plopped on the floor with a thumping sound, followed by the metallic ring of the axe blade still embedded in the decapitated creature's head.

I plucked my dagger from Gruterrig's bleeding, shattered eye, and raced to where Xycanthia braced herself against the south wall of her feasting hall, trying to recover from the Vampyre's Bane mixture that I had thrown into her face.

I grabbed her by the throat and slammed her against the wall, holding my dagger over her heart. "Now, you are going to die; and Ghormanteia's death will follow!" I growled, drawing back my blade to drive into her heart.

"Ghormanteia? That bastard, Ghormanteia?" she choked.

"So, you fiends all know one another?" I grunted, tightening my grip on her throat.

The power of the phantom-charged armor was so great that even with her daemonic strength, she could not break my grip.

"He sent me here. Exiled me here. Like you. It is but a jest to him. Next time he will kill you," Xycanthia coughed out as I released the pressure on her throat.

I drew back with my dagger and repositioned it in my fist, holding the blade upward to her throat and grabbing her by her lovely crimson locks.

"Tell me what you know—and quickly—before I change my mind, daemoness!"

"I knew you weren't from this world when I first laid eyes on you, Karnov. It was he who sent you here, wasn't it?"

"Aye, blood-wench," I answered, choosing to say as little as possible until I knew what she was about.

"Ghormanteia endeavors to expand his kingdom throughout the world you know. Once he has subjugated it, he will move into other worlds, like this one. I see you have the spell of the Cosmic Ice available to you. You must be in league with my bitch sister, D'vartha. I heard you say her name when you entered my abode. I thought she had sent you to kill me; such is the love between us," Xycanthia informed me.

"Your infamy is known throughout the kingdoms of this strange world," I calmly replied. "I sought to redden my blade in your daemon-tainted blood that I might return to Ghormanteia's lair, and avenge the murders of my wife and son."

"How did you end up here, Karnov?" Xycanthia asked.

"I entered Ghormanteia's lair by the Cosmic Ice," I told her. "There was an orgy in his chamber and they were burning the yellow lotus. My thoughts were scattered by the fumes of the drug, and Ghormanteia had his giant pet snake coil about me and my horse. I woke up galloping on my mount in this strange world."

"White Wyrm! Ghormanteia had the serpent drip its mystical venom onto you and exiled you to Tchorthsis—this world where you now are. He did it as a jest. If you return, he will have White Wyrm swallow you and vomit you back out, turning you into his vampyre slave; or he will simply kill you outright. He knew you were coming. He was prepared for you. Did you notice him peering into any object when you first arrived?"

"He was looking into an orb that he set aside. I placed no importance on gewgaws at the time. I had murder on my mind!" I ejected.

"That orb was the Eye of Orlock. It is the eye one of the most powerful vampyre mages that ever existed, set in crystal. With it, Ghormanteia can see several minutes into the future. He will know you are coming just like the first time. Listen! I have a score to settle with that mangy bastard for exiling me here with no way back, and I want the Eye of Orlock! You want Ghormanteia dead! Both things can be accomplished if we combine our resources."

I gripped my dagger hard in my right hand. I knew better than to trust vampyres. I looked at Qoulitiax who had been silently standing by, listening to every word. Qoulitiax squinted her eyes and nodded her head at me.

I turned my attention back to Xycanthia. "Do you agree not to harm me or Qoulitiax?"

"Aye, Karnov. I agree," said Xycanthia.

I looked at my companion, and Qoulitiax again nodded her head at me.

"Do you not agree that a vampyre is full of cunning?" she asked, adding, "And is that not a woman's weapon by nature?"

I lowered my dagger and sheathed it.

"Very good. I have a plan. Listen!" Xycanthia hissed.

Book III
By Byron A. Roberts

Chapter I
The Scheme of the Crimson Seductress

Xycanthia's viridescent eyes widened as she fixed me with a baleful, fever-bright glare. "Hearken to me, Karnov, traverser of worlds," the vampyress hissed, her pearlescent fangs gleaming behind her fulsome ruby lips. "You desire vengeance upon the foul Ghormanteia, as do I. By all the black gods of Chaos, I would see that thrice-cursed fiend flayed by the searing light of a thousand suns for the base treachery he perpetrated against me!"

I folded my powerful arms across my steel-clad chest and smiled mirthlessly at the lissom succubus seething before me. "Aye, we have common cause, blood-witch. I seek his head, you seek the Eye of Orlock. Pray tell what perfidious plot roils within your malefic mind. Speak quickly, lest you desire another draught of my Vampyre's Bane!"

The crimson-tressed vampyress sighed wearily, her alabastrine brow furrowing. "You have discovered to your cost that the hoary spells woven by my sister D'vartha are not proof against Ghormanteia's insidious power. Alone, that fulgid shell of eldritch ice which girds your hulking frame is insufficient to counter his yellow lotus mist and the venom of his ophidian White Wyrm! Something other than your ensorcelled steel is required to bring that devil low!"

"Then what do you suggest?" I growled. "Out with it, for my time is short, as is my patience!"

Xycanthia's sensual lips curled in a cruel smile, her eburnean flesh shimmering in the wan torchlight. "I am the key to victory," she breathed. "Together we shall cross the void between worlds and wreak our vengeance. My exile in this blighted realm must end. By allying my arcane power with yours, we can sunder the tenebrous shackles which bind me here and voyage beyond the dimensional threshold. Our covenant shall be potent enough to rend the veil and bear us both through the portal. We shall journey through the frozen maelstrom and confront the bastard with steel and spellcraft!"

"Feh!" I gnarred irately. "The cankerous dog would see us coming by peering into that cursed bloody jewel!"

"Nay, Karnov! My magicks can negate his ill-born power of temporal foresight, robbing him of that fiendish advantage and evening the odds immeasurably!"

"And what of that accursed ivory serpent he commands?" I rumbled. "How do we slay that vile abomination?"

Xycanthia's beguiling smile widened. "Leave that to me. I can weave the necessary spells to safeguard you from its envenomed maw and empower your azure steel to rend its scaly hide! Once that fell beast is dead, we shall avenge ourselves upon Ghormanteia!"

"And all you seek is the black orb he covets?" I asked guardedly. "This arcane Eye of Orlock?"

"Of course, my dear Karnov," the beauteous blood-witch whispered. "You have my word."

Scowling, I turned to fair Qoulitiax, my flaxen-tressed companion, who skulked beside me eyeing the black-clad woman warily. "What think you, lass?"

Qoulitiax frowned, regarding the sinuous vampyress with naked suspicion. "Why do you desire the orb so desperately, night-bitch?" she snapped. "What power does it truly possess?"

Xycanthia interlaced her slender fingers and shrugged. "It is merely an object of great historical and ancestral significance to my kind. The Eye of Orlock, arch-mage of the ancient Alunai! Granted, it bestows a minor boon of limited foresight, but scant little else. At any rate, it is far too valuable an artefact to be held by a base revenant such as Ghormanteia!"

I studied the aquiline countenance of Qoulitiax intently. "Well? I know all too well that the wiles of a woman can be the ruination of both beggar and king. But mayhap you can see through the veil of her deception, and fathom whether any duplicitous thoughts lurk within her inhuman mind."

Qoulitiax sighed, brushing an errant strand of golden hair from her delicate brow. "It seems we have no choice but to ally ourselves with her, Karnov."

"Splendid!" Xycanthia exclaimed, her voice colder than the north wind. "We should waste no time! Our journey must begin at once! But first, you must fully empower yourself, my brave Phantom Rider! You shall require all your arcane might to summon the ice-bound portal and overcome the spell of exile which binds me to this desolate realm. Aye, Karnov… you must anoint yourself with the blood of my darkling kin!"

With a wave of her snow-pale hand, Xycanthia summoned three vampyric myrmidons from the shadows of the glooming chamber. The diminutive, cloaked figures glided silently from the blackness like supine wraiths, obediently assembling before me. Their gaunt and pallid faces displayed no hint of animation, their lifeless eyes gazing mournfully into the brooding bitumen void.

"Now, Karnov…" the darksome woman whispered. "Accept this sacrifice. Glut the maw of your sorcerous raiment!"

I needed no further encouragement. My azure blade hissed from its scabbard and flashed like an adamantine talon in the guttering half-light. The chalybeous steel clove the first of the fiends like a scythe through the summer field, sundering its cadaverous flesh. Blood erupted from the riven corpse of the creature and a sapphirean glow immediately flared along the honed edge of the sword. My scintillant weapon sang again and the second vampyre swiftly collapsed to the stone floor, its vulpine face a viscid and mangled ruin. The third dolent entity then duly received the pitiless blessing of my searing blade with wordless gratitude, its malodorous innards spilling from its ankylosed frame. A cerulean aura of sorcerous energy instantly enveloped me, illumining the chamber with a blinding radiance. Suddenly, I was surrounded by the writhing incorporeal shades of the epigones I had slain, their spectral essences flowing into my war-scored thews. The time-lost glyphs of the Cosmic Ice danced before my eyes with a fulgid splendour, swiftly searing their pictographic forms into my frost-cloaked mantle as the relucent armour of eldritch ice blazed about my body, far more brightly than before. The great frozen helm shone ever more radiantly upon my head and my rune-etched blade pulsed with a coruscant brilliance. The ghostly forms of the slain fiends surged within my armour, rippling across the surface of my mail hauberk and steel cuirass like blue mercury as pale wisps of dun-white vapour rose from my ice-bound frame in writhing tendrils. I hefted my crackling sword in predatory rapture.

"Behold," I bellowed exultantly, "The Phantom-Clad Rider of the Cosmic Ice is reborn!"

"You stand now at full potency!" shouted Xycanthia gleefully. "Never before have you served as the vessel to power of this magnitude! Now, weave the enchantment to rend the veil that we may return to Duros Zuil. Bear us hence to Castle Thornhaven with all speed!"

"To me, Wrathmane!" I thundered, brandishing my howling yard of ice-veiled steel.

With a thunderclap and a storm-wrought flash of azure light, my heavily muscled steed crashed through the sturdy oaken doors of Xycanthia's feasting hall and reared before us, his sinewy flanks once again girt by the same icy cocoon of sorcerous energy which encased my own body. I vaulted to my mount's broad back and swept the slender form of Qoulitiax up to sit astride my saddle behind me, whereupon her trembling arms instantly encircled my waist. "Fear not, lady," I boomed. "The Cosmic Ice shall not harm thee on the journey, not while you reside within my protective aura. Once this foul deed of vengeance is done, I shall bear thee safely back to your father's court in Turnia, and by the gods you'll have a rousing tale to tell indeed!"

"I pray you are right, Karnov," whispered Qoulitiax. "I have no desire to tarry long in the lair of Ghormanteia!"

"Take this," I said, drawing my long-bladed cerulean dagger from its sheath and pressing it into the girl's delicate hand. "It is imbued with the spectral power of my enchantment. When we cross the threshold into that seething viper's nest, dismount and stay hidden as best you can. But if it comes to it, use this blade and aim for the heart of whatever vile thing assails you."

"Enough talk!" snapped Xycanthia. "To the castle of my nemesis, and red retribution!"

Leaning sharply in my caesious saddle, I swept my broadsword downward in a lambent arc, preparing to carve the fell symbol of the tainted chalice which would rend the gossamer veil between worlds and open the frozen pathway to my grim destination. Swiftly I drove the glowing blade into the floor of Xycanthia's feasting hall, etching the arcane sigil unerringly into the stained tiles. The honed steel scored the stone as effortlessly as a butcher's cleaver cutting through a bloodied carcass and plumes of azure fire erupted from the furrows in the black marble. And so it was that I summoned the vortex of Cosmic Ice which would transport us from the gloomy environs of Xycanthia's keep directly to the sanguineous charnel-pit which men called Castle Thornhaven…

Chapter II
Vengeance in the Citadel of the Damned

Untrammelled carnage reigned in the black hall of Ghormanteia. Scant seconds after we had surged forth through the cerulean maelstrom of eldritch ice, the battle was joined and my frost-veiled blade was dark with corrupted blood. "Didn't see that coming did you, devil?" I bellowed to the vampyre lord as I hefted my ensorcelled steel triumphantly.

With an ireful equine shriek, Wrathmane reared and hammered his iron-shod hooves downward, dashing the brains of a vampyric acolyte to the stone floor in a slurry of grey and crimson gore.

To my left I spied Xycanthia, now fully transmogrified into her grotesque inhuman guise, rending the throat of a bestial lackey with her searing talons. The vile plumes of the yellow lotus which permeated the cavernous chamber were now wholly ineffectual, negated by the spells of the seductress as she had promised. I could not see Qoulitiax from my current vantage point, but I assumed she had taken cover safely within the shadows as I had bidden her.

My ancestral blade clove the snarling head from the shoulders of a misshapen creature and I instantly felt its phantasmagorical essence flow into the azure armour which crackled about my frame. Thrice more my sword hewed through vampyric flesh, and the souls of the undead flew instantly to my enchanted aura like lambent moths drawn unerringly to an icy flame. Securing my shield to Wrathmane's steel-plated crupper, I levelled my gaze at the vile master of Castle Thornhaven.

"Ghormanteia!" I thundered. "I come for thee!"

I saw the vampyre-lord scowl, his pallid and toothsome countenance creasing horrifically. His purple silken robes billowed and one of his clawed hands scrabbled for the hidden mechanism concealed upon the arm of his slime-flecked throne.

"Not this time!" I hissed, pulling a hidden bodkin dagger from the ornate hilt of my sword. With preternatural speed, I hurled the slender stiletto across the chamber and it struck home unerringly, embedding itself within the fiend's sinewy forearm. Ghormanteia shrieked in pain, the vile keening sound cresting the cacophonous wave of the battle's din. In an instant I had vaulted from Wrathmane's saddle and bounded across the hall to my darksome nemesis, laying hold of his fibrous thews and hurling him from the throne's black dais. And yet to my dismay, I realized he had still somehow managed to activate the hoary device and his regal seat swiftly began to descend into the depths of the bone-strewn floor with a great grinding and groaning sound. But this time at least, the odious devil was no longer seated upon the throne to flee the darkling chamber! I spun to the foul-featured aberration and levelled the point of my glowing sword at his throat. "We have unfinished business, you and I."

Ghormanteia grimaced and wrenched my bloodied bodkin from his scored forearm, letting it clatter heedlessly to the black floor. Then the vampire-lord's hideous chiropteran face contorted into a vile parody of a smile as viscid gouts of slaver dripped from his fanged maw. "I see you have brought the beauteous Xycanthia with you!" he rasped. "That explains why the Eye of Orlock's gift of foresight has been rendered impotent, if naught else."

"Aye! Your sorcery is nullified, devil of Aschorzotha! As is the foul kiss of the yellow lotus!"

"Well, no matter," Ghormanteia seethed. "Two lost souls returned from exile. Splendid! The conspirators can die together!"

A great hissing sound suddenly arose at my back and I turned to see the vast and sinuous form of the White Wyrm ascending from the aphotic pit, its scaly flesh encoiled around the now rising throne. I lifted my coruscant blade just as the beast's ruby maw yawned open and a torrent of yellow venom lashed forth. The searing ichor spattered my sword and armour, bubbling upon the surface of my ensorcelled raiment.

“Your cursed venom will not avail you, pit-spawn!” I bellowed. “Now, suffer the judgement of steel!”

I arced my blade toward the beast’s alabaster flesh and the honed edge bit deep into its writhing ophidian form. A blossom of green blood erupted from its riven hide and the White Wyrm shrieked in sibilant agony. Instantly, the foul creature struck, driving its hooked fangs into my lambent pauldron with terrible ferocity. The withering stench of the beast’s acrid breath assailed me and white-hot pain lanced through my body. The wyrm’s great scimitar teeth sank deeper into my armour and its pallid undulating girth inexorably began to encoil me in a vice-like grip.

“No!” I snarled. “I will not fall before this abyssal abomination!”

And as I uttered that oath, a sublime rage enveloped my mind and my ice-bound armour flared momentarily brighter. Tendrils of smoke began to billow forth from the vile serpent’s venomous maw and a heartbeat later it abruptly released its death-hold upon me, rearing backwards with its curved fangs and forked tongue ablaze with blue fire.

“Feel now the wrath of the Cosmic Ice!” I thundered, driving my sword upwards towards the creature’s scaly head. My blade pierced the wyrm’s lower jaw and with all my might I thrust the azure steel further into its muculent white flesh. With a resonant crack and a gout of green blood, my sword emerged slick and steaming from the transfixed head of the monster. A great tremor ran through the beast’s sinuous body and I dragged my befouled sword free of its riven skull. Before the dread White Wyrm could fall, I summoned all my strength and hacked the beast’s scaly head from its ophidian body. Hot green blood spilled forth from the creature’s twitching bulk in glutinous waves and its ravaged head tumbled gruesomely to the black floor of the chamber.

“Verminous beast!” I growled. “Thus has your filth been cleansed from the face of creation!” I lifted the visor of my crested helm and inhaled deeply, momentarily savouring my victory over the serpentine titan.

Suddenly, I was struck brutally from behind and the air was driven painfully from my lungs by the force of the impact. A powerful sinewy arm encircled my throat and filthy talons scrabbled desperately for my eyes. Ghormanteia hissed and tightened his hold upon me, his preternatural strength seeking to constrict the very life from my body in a crushing, iron grip.

"'Tis such a pity that my pet has failed to rid me of your accursed presence," he rasped malefically. "My vassal Nesadomntha will be most aggrieved to learn of the beast's demise. Well, no matter! It clearly falls to me to finish the job!"

I discerned the gruesome sound of distending flesh and stretching sinew and knew instantly that Ghormanteia was commencing the transmogrification into his bestial winged form. The devil was evidently seeking the tenfold increase in strength and durability which the fiendish transformation would afford him. "Not today," I rumbled, and drove my helmeted head backward into Ghormanteia's pallid brow with all the might I could muster. There came the unmistakable crack of yielding cartilage and the vampyre-lord abruptly released his hold upon me, collapsing heavily to the stone floor. I spun and regarded the fallen revenant, noting with a surge of satisfaction that his vile face was now a ruinous mass of viscid blood and fractured bone. Instantly, I seized hold of the insensate fiend's voluminous robes with my gore-flecked gauntlet and hauled him unceremoniously to his feet.

"Know this," I growled. "The enchantment of my spectral armour will prevent your transmutation as long as you are within my grasp. Now it is time to pay for your crimes, foul one!"

I glanced about the chamber and witnessed Xycanthia still engaged in battle with the remnants of Ghormanteia's vampyric brood, her leathern wings spattered with blood, ragged ribbons of torn flesh hanging from her slender talons. Close by, mighty Wrathmane's ice-shod hooves trampled another fiend's skull to noisome pulp and the noble steed reared, snorting in primal triumph. A cruel grin crossed my face and I turned my attention back to Ghormanteia.

"For unleashing your virulent plague upon my land and corrupting my wife and son, I condemn you to death. A death from which there will be no resurrection. I shall have my vengeance this day. And not soon enough has it come."

"Wait!" Ghormanteia rasped, blood bubbling from his black lips. "What bargain did you strike with Xycanthia? What does she seek for aiding thee?"

"Only your sorcerous bauble," I replied, tightening my grip upon my sword. "And her freedom."

Dark laughter welled in the vampyre's throat. "Only the Eye of Orlock? There is more to this artefact than she has disclosed, human." Ghormanteia produced the eldritch orb from the sleeve of his robe and held it aloft before me, the glimmer of the chamber's torchlight reflected in its obsidian depths. "This is but one of Orlock's eyes! Xycanthia has the other! When both are combined, her power will increase immeasurably. She will possess the might to enslave a myriad worlds and breed a new race of demonic, blood-bloated fiends!"

I frowned and pulled the aberrant creature closer. "An insidious goal you share with her, so I hear. Pray continue, devil."

"Then hearken to me," Ghormanteia spat. "The blood-witch and I battled over these orbs centuries ago, a conflict which ended in bitter stalemate. Ever since, we have plotted and schemed to seize control of both artefacts. Six score and ten years ago, I exiled her to the realm of Tchorthsis, awaiting the day that our ageless war would inevitably resume. She manipulates you for her own nefarious ends, deluded human! The traitoress must not wrest this orb from me!"

"An interesting tale, to be sure," I rumbled. "If what you say is true, then rest assured neither of you shall possess the Eyes. Now, I grow weary of your accursed prattle. Prepare to die!"

"Fool!" shrieked Ghormanteia, struggling desperately in my spell-forged grasp. "You dare threaten me? I am immortal! I am the Bane of the Alunai, the Master of the Thulagantar, the Scourge of the Thirteen Hells! To your flaccid and mewling race, I am like unto a king!"

"Indeed?" I growled, hefting my crackling blade. "Then I am Karnov, Breaker of Kings."

And with that, I swept the vampyre-lord's head cleanly from his body.

* * *

My ice-bound raiment was replete with undead souls, the essence of Ghormanteia empowering me to levels of hitherto unfathomed might.

The battle in Castle Thornhaven had ceased and the carnage had all but abated. The ravaged bodies of slain vampyres and acolytes littered the stone floor of the chamber and silence brooded over the charnel-keep like a hoary tomb. Suddenly I heard the flurry of leathern wings behind me and I spun to see Xycanthia emerging from the shadows, once more clad in her alluring human guise. Her viridescent eyes sparkled and a cruel smile curled her lips.

"Well done, Karnov," purred Xycanthia. "The vile fiend is dead. I have kept my part of the bargain. Now, you must keep yours. Where is the Eye of Orlock?"

I smiled back at the crimson-tressed seductress. "This?" I said, holding aloft the fulgid, crystal orb. "Such a tumult over so petty a thing. Mayhap I shall keep it and sell it at the bazaars. I hear the merchants of Klahr-Atoch pay decent gold for unusual gems."

The smile abruptly faded from Xycanthia's face. "You cannot!" Our deal was struck! You must not renege!"

"Enough treachery!" I spat. "There are two Eyes! You did not tell me you possessed the other. Nor did you enlighten me as to the fell power that they are capable of bestowing!"

"What lies did the foul Ghormanteia tell you?" Xycanthia cried, moving slowly toward me. "Anything to save his feculent skin, I'll wager. Give me the orb and our covenant will be complete."

"Why? So that I may merely trade his tyrannical aspirations for yours? I think not."

Xycanthia fixed me with her emerald eyes, a lambent glow radiating from their shimmering depths. "You will do my bidding, Karnov," she said, her silken voice husky and hypnotic. "You have no choice but to obey."

A sensation of opiate bliss suddenly enveloped me and my vision began to blur. Xycanthia's viridescent eyes burned brighter and my limbs began to feel heavy as a great mantle of weariness swiftly enshrouded my body. Powerless, I watched my hand slowly proffer the orb to the leering vampyress.

"Yes," Xycanthia hissed, reaching reverentially out toward the Eye of Orlock. "You have done well, Karnov. By way of a reward, your death will be mercifully swift. Or mayhap I should bestow upon thee the dark blessings of the Red Thirst, so that you may stalk the night at my side for all eternity, becoming the very thing that you revile the most? How divinely amusing that would be!"

An eldritch moment of utter stillness and absolute silence descended upon the shadowed chamber, as if the eternal heart of time itself had ceased to beat for one single, immemorial instant. Then, with a flash of azure light, the point of a dagger suddenly erupted forth from Xycanthia's chest and her spell of beguilement was instantly shattered.

The black-clad temptress gasped, gazing incredulously down at the point of glowing blue steel which had abruptly emerged from her alabastrine bosom. Without a word, Xycanthia slumped to the stone floor and lay still, a pool of dark blood widening beneath her lifeless form like a great stygian blossom.

My vision cleared swiftly and I beheld Qoulitiax holding the blood-stained dagger, her delicate brow arching. "You did say aim for the heart," she said with a wry smile.

"Well done, lass!" I boomed. "That viperous blood-witch nearly had me enthralled!"

I knelt and searched the folds of Xycanthia's black robes, my hands tracing the contours of her cold and swiftly disintegrating body. Finally, I located what I sought... the second Eye of Orlock. I stood upright and gazed intently at the twin sinistrous orbs glimmering in my hand. Then, I cast both gems to the floor and crushed them to darkling shards beneath my icy heel.

"She was a wretched wench," I mused. "I must confess that I suspected some manner of duplicity on her part. I just didn't know precisely what form it would take until the end."

"Never trust a vampyre," spat Qoulitiax with disdain.

"Words to live by," I assented. "In truth, I never intended to allow her the orb, so ultimately our deception was mutual. And yet it vexes me that I could not claim her black soul, for the death-blow was not dealt by my hand. Ah well, mayhap her malign spirit now wanders some diabolical undead purgatory."

"We can but hope," muttered Qoulitiax.

Wrathmane then cantered dutifully from the shadows, his mighty hooves dark with the blood of slaughtered fiends and his steel chanfron and crinet scored with a myriad deep furrows wrought by vampyric talons.

Qoulitiax stepped closer to me and shuddered. "Can we leave this blighted place now, Karnov?" she breathed.

"Aye, lass!" I said. "My task here is done. My vengeance is complete. I shall bear thee home, as promised. But before we journey to your father's distant court, we have one final stop to make. We must pay a visit to the blood-kin of Xycanthia!"

Chapter III
Return to the Garden of Unearthly Delights

We traversed the fulgent vortex of the Cosmic Ice, surging through the frozen maelstrom with unparalleled speed. All around us, fleeting images of other worlds shimmered in the spectral shadows of the labyrinth. I gazed in awe as we thundered past a seemingly endless vista of strange and exotic domains; ancient lands wherein black ziggurats brooded, coruscant realms boasting splendid cities which proffered their bejewelled spires to the heavens, and a myriad other darkling worlds which radiated a far more sinister and alien aspect. For a scant second, I glimpsed a desolate scarlet desert studded with mighty crystalline pyramids, then a bleak and blighted landscape above which towered colossal statues hewn to resemble terrifying ophidian titans. At length, the familiar terrain of Duros Zuil became visible in the depths of the lucent icescape and I began to rein my steed to a halt. For several harrowing moments, the vortex spiralling around us surged ever more violently and a colossal din akin to the crashing of a storm-wracked ocean filled our ears. Then, the interdimensional portal abruptly vanished and we stood upon the barren heath not five miles from D'vartha's arboreal abode. Plumes of icy vapour rose languidly from Wrathmane's flanks and the sheen of eldritch frost which had formed upon my armour during the journey swiftly began to dissipate.

"That... was amazing!" cried Qoulitiax, shifting excitedly in the saddle behind me. "Even more spectacular than the last time!"

"A voyage through the heart of the Cosmic Ice does tend to be somewhat memorable," I replied as I spurred my mount onto the nearby roadway. "Now, let us call upon a rather peculiar enchantress of my acquaintance!"

* * *

"I bear a gift for thee, D'vartha," I said to the red-haired witch as I gazed down at her from Wrathmane's broad back.

"Is that so, Phantom Rider?" D'vartha replied, driving her iron tipped pitchfork into the black soil of her sorcerous garden. Her green eyes narrowed disdainfully as she beheld Qoulitiax mounted behind me in the saddle. "Not a lover's token, I assume?"

I threw a bloodied bundle of sackcloth to D'vartha's feet and watched as she quickly gathered up and unbound its hempen folds. A delighted smile then illumined the witch's face as she pulled the severed head of Xycanthia from the sack and held it aloft by a long strand of its still lustrous red hair.

"My dear sister!" D'vartha cried gleefully, staring into the grey, cadaverous face of the dead vampyress. "By the dark gods, she's never looked better! Where in the world did you encounter her?"

"Not in this world at all," I replied. "We met in the far-flung realm of Tchorthsis and briefly became allies, for we were both exiled there by Ghormanteia. But I fear her traitorous nature soured the relationship and our covenant was fleeting."

Cruel laughter sang from the witch's lips and she fixed me with an ireful glare. "Ah yes, treachery was always Xycanthia's way. There was no love lost between us, I assure you. She was a vile bitch to me when we were neophytes in the Welkin Coven, nigh on three centuries past."

"Truly? You are older than you look," I muttered wryly.

"Why, thank you, my valiant paladin," the witch beamed, idly twirling her crimson locks. "I do strive to maintain my youthful appearance. At any rate, as Xycanthia and I grew to womanhood, our paths inevitably diverged as she delved deeply into ever more malign sources of arcane power. My wayward sister ultimately sought the dark blessings of vampyrism. I neglected to mention her. Pray forgive me."

"Fear not, shamaness," I said. "Ghormanteia is dead, and I bear thee no ill will. After all, it was your sorcery which imbued me with the power to wreak my ravening vengeance upon that arch-fiend."

"And that power is yours for eternity, Karnov," D'vartha said. "The question must now be posed. How will you wield it henceforth?"

I sighed wearily. "The vile devil who took my loved ones from me is no more. But there are others akin to him out there. Countless acolytes of the black virulence remain at large. I will hunt them. Wherever they lurk and breed throughout the myriad worlds, I will track them and render unto them the purifying judgement of the Phantom-Clad Rider. The labyrinthine web of the Cosmic Ice is mine to traverse. Although its true nature is beyond my ken, I am certain of one thing… this is what I was born for. This is my destiny."

"Well said, Karnov Ice-Blade," D'vartha said solemnly. "Across the aeons, many others have borne the burden of this power. It is a lonely and desolate path, full of carnage and sorrow. Should you require further aid, you have but to seek me here." A lascivious smile then crept across the witch's beauteous face and her green eyes sparkled mischievously. "I can offer you many kinds of succour."

I grinned wolfishly and reined Wrathmane away from the witch and her eldritch garden. "Of that I'm sure! Farewell, D'vartha. We shall meet again!"

Wrathmane's iron-shod hooves beat a rhythmic tattoo upon the mossy earth as I rode away through the forest of gnarled and shadowed trees, leaving D'vartha's hovel ever farther in the sylvan distance. I rode in silence, lost in my grim reverie and sombre contemplation as I reflected upon all that had transpired in the short time since my fateful return from the battlefield of Orobos Sandus. Sullenly, I pondered all that I had gained and mourned for all that I had lost. At length, we emerged from the arboreal vault of the deep woods and onto the dusty road once more.

"That witch fair resembles her vile sister," sighed Qoulitiax as she gazed up at the brooding, dusk-painted sky.

I nodded. "That she does! But thankfully, their souls are as starkly different as night and day."

"Is it now time to return to my homeland, Karnov?"

"Aye, lass," I replied. "It is. But my spectral power has waned during our sojourn here. In order to conjure the ice-bound portal which leads to your father's realm, I shall need to slake my armour's thirst once more. Many fiends still roam this land. Their iniquitous souls will suffice to empower me. We shall hunt, fair lady. Once again shall I blacken my blade with the impure blood of the undead. The oath is sworn! The vow proclaimed! Onward to righteous ruin and the harrowing of the damned!"

And I spurred Wrathmane west towards the setting sun.

And so it was that Karnov returned the long-imperilled daughter of Count Magne to her home in distant Turnia, steadfastly refusing the bounty of gold and gems which the grateful nobleman duly offered as a reward for the rescue of fair Qoulitiax. Bidding farewell to his beauteous charge, Karnov rode many leagues to the east, compelled by disquieting rumours of an ancient vampyric demigod newly resurrected by a nefarious coven of necromancers far beyond the frontiers of the distant Chang-Liam Empire. But that is another story...

Karnov: Phantom-Clad Rider of the Cosmic Ice

Episode II
Bane of the Necromancer's Brood

Book I
By Matthew Knight

Chapter I
Phantom-Clad Retribution (Clash with Earthly Demonic Scourges)

Hanging lamps poured an amber glow of honey and sulphur upon the crude streets as cold night-winds from surrounding mountain ranges howled like spectral wolves, blowing my heavy black cloak and chilling the metal shield upon my back. My armored steed and fellow companion Wrathmane's hoofs clicked upon the dirt and cobblestone road that led to a familiar inn at the center of town. It was there I was heading to try to gather some information—as well as have an ale or two, and warm my bones by their hearth. I had returned to Duros Zuil, and the journey had been long.

Although aided by the cosmic gateways, due to the recent destruction of Lord Ghormanteia and his haunted estate by my hand over a year ago, the nearby portal that used to exist was now inactive; therefore, I was forced to trek all the way from the nearest one I could traverse, which was many miles away. Even delayed by this small inconvenience, I remained ever grateful for the sorcerous gift which allowed me to dimensionally travel the earth, and fight with uncanny might against those I hunted.

I'd spent the last year fighting evil in the Far East. Gaining status of royalty in the Golden City of Thuram Kholn, I was treated as a king after vanquishing a deadly threat to their land using the secrets of the Cosmic Ice; a power over the undead which only I possessed. After my great victory, I spent some time cleansing the "golden" city of its remaining corruption—that of the non-supernatural kind. Within a short time, I had dethroned their tyrannical rulers, reorganized their unjust government, and banished their newly-established sinister religion. Afterwards, I spent several weeks enjoying the fine luxuries the place had to offer, while keeping an eye on things.

One night while asleep upon a silk-clad couch, drunk on the juice of the purple dedeim, and lustfully entwined in the arms of lovely maidens whom I had freed from the nation's cruel slavery, a dark vision came to me in a dream.

In my drugged slumber (the dedeim is known for inducing profound trance), I saw a hazy image of people gathered in the marketplace of my former homeland. They were going about their business, as usual. Farmers were selling livestock, young maids mended quilts and jerkins while tool traders and weaponsmiths dealt across wooden booths. I saw old neighbors, kinfolk, and others I knew and loved in my former years; all laughing, trading and bargaining in the town square—just as I'd remembered from old times. It was quite a familiar spectacle and a pleasant reminder of home.

The peaceful scene suddenly became horrifying as a host of obscene creatures came rushing into the square and began wreaking havoc. They appeared to be vampyres, but afflicted with an otherworldly, cosmic taint. Naked and apparently sexless, their skin had a greenish hue. From their large heads, flailing tentacles writhed in lieu of hair. Their eyes were large and red without pupils, and their noses were like those of cats. Slavering mouths gaped wide, displaying long fangs like those of the undead I was accustomed to, and they drooled green saliva all about as they rushed in.

The monsters attacked the townsfolk mercilessly. I watched as screaming young girls were ravaged and had their blood sucked dry. Some of the men attempted to fight back, and had their jugulars ripped out, or were dismembered before being devoured. The things were fast and powerful. The alien vampyres even ravished the livestock as they fed upon any living thing in sight. A great hatred arose in me as the entire place became a bloodbath, and all those I recognized and loved had been slain.

The vision then faded to darkness. When I opened my eyes, a spectral image appeared before me: the transparent apparition of a dark wraith clothed in tattered black rags with its face hidden beneath a cowl hovered in the air before my couch.

"Karnov..." the wraith hissed. "I bring you news of a great menace to your land. The vision you just witnessed was no mere hallucination. This event was real and others like it are taking place every day. A new breed of vampyre has arrived in Duros Zuil."

I was unable to move or say anything, and the women slumbering in my arms remained sleeping as if completely unaware of the supernatural visit.

"You must return to your homeland," hissed the shade. "It is up to you to defeat this new threat. Remember, Karnov—your vengeance can never truly be achieved as long as these fiends still roam the land."

The phantom faded into thin air, and I was released from its spell.

The next day I left Thuram Kholn in haste. I knew not who the ghostly visitor was or if the vision I saw was real, but I had to find out for myself—for if the undead were about in Duros Zuil, it would be their fate to die by my yard of spectral steel.

The road brought me to the town square. This was an open space of cobblestone street, where the locals gathered to do business daily. It was also where the horrible scene took place in my dream. There were street lanterns burning but no one in sight. Only a few of the booths and store carts that were usually set up still stood. The rest were either gone or lay in ruins. The shops surrounding the area were all closed, and some were boarded shut—all except the Wolf's Bane Inn which was lit up and seemed to be doing business.

I was about to dismount and head inside before the door opened and two figures stepped out. They were young men, drunk and laughing. One wore a brown, brimmed hat and a long coat, while the other was clad in a vest of thick gray fur and had a premature moustache. I urged Wrathmane to step back into the shadows in order to remain unnoticed by the cackling boys.

"Did you see that slut in there that Jondar Barthulle was drooling over?" the one who wore the hat slurred.

"Aye, he'd be right at home with that one," replied the other. "I've seen a sow or two in his stockyard with tits that size!"

The lads ruptured in hysterics as they stumbled across the empty plaza together.

"I suppose we'd best not make too much noise in the street—lest those things are about…" said the lad with the moustache.

"We might want to," the other replied. "I hear they suck even better than that whore in there!"

Their cachinnation commenced.

"Silence," a voice adjured.

The boys hushed suddenly, as a figure now stood before them in the lantern light. It was a tall man dressed in noble garb. His face was pale and he had long, straight hair as black as night. He wore an ebon tunic of lace and silk with ruffled sleeves beneath a polished jet steel breastplate that had a royal crest etched upon it in gold. Flowing down his back was a decorated crimson cape that spanned to the ground. He wore ornately armored greaves and gauntlets of polished bronze and onyx. At his side hung a rapier in an elegant scabbard that looked to be a weapon of antiquity. He must have moved incredibly stealthily, as he had come upon the youths completely unaware in the empty street, and even I did not notice his approach.

"It is not a laughing matter." The man spoke in a deep, solemn voice and had a foreign accent I did not recognize. "Had you or your loved ones been victims of the attacks, you would not jest so. Be on your way before you awaken them with your foolish chatter."

The boys said nothing, but regarded the stranger with surprise and awe. I found his appearance peculiar, and I wondered what a person of his obvious stature could be doing in Duros Zuil.

Suddenly, the eyes of the moustached young man widened. He looked beyond the newcomer into the dark street opening behind where he stood.

"It's too late!" he said and pointed.

The distant sound of a running mob, accompanied by an uncanny growling and hissing was heard coming from where the boy indicated. Then they appeared in the torchlight—a dozen of the same creatures I saw in my vision: naked, undead, green humanoid things with flailing tentacles writhing from their heads. Their mouths were agape, baring deadly fangs as they rushed toward the startled humans.

The dark-haired man drew his sword. "Be gone!" he shouted to the youths who ran away without hesitation.

Quickly, I spurred Wrathmane out of the shadows and into the square.

The pale foreigner had already begun hacking at the creatures. He stabbed the first fiend through the heart, causing black ichor to spray. The thing howled in pain before it fell to the ground, dying.

Wrathmane galloped full speed toward the hideous throng. As one of the creatures lunged toward me, from my mount I swung my sword in a whirling arc, severing its tentacled head. As soon as the putrid thing's body hit the cobblestones, its soul was released. The tainted spirit visibly flew like a will-o'-the-wisp into my armor, and was absorbed—thus my cosmic transformation was initiated; the blood of the vampyre had activated my supernatural powers. A glowing blue, icy substance encased my rune-etched armor, sword, shield and helm, as the ghostly aura of the creature I absorbed now swirled and writhed along my frame. I felt a cold sensation run through my veins and my muscles raged with strength.

I urged Wrathmane—who had also become empowered by the Cosmic Ice, and clad in a glowing mass of frozen spirit-mail—into the mass of deadly brutes. One was crushed beneath his silver-shod hooves, while I leaned down and thrust my sword into the chest of another, driving the blade down its torso and into its belly, spilling foul green entrails onto the street.

When the stranger noticed my coming, he looked over toward me and nodded once while fighting. Surprisingly he seemed not amazed or startled by my appearance. He moved with an almost supernatural quickness, as he continued to surgically thrust his ornate blade through the hearts of each creature he encountered. I saw that it was not in the exact place a human heart would be—but this stranger knew precisely where it was.

I leapt from Wrathmane's back to join in close combat with the remaining fiends. As I joined in the fray, their sharp, slimy claws swiped at me, only to be pulled away as they wailed in agony the moment they touched my haunted armor. I sliced the head off another and felt a euphoric ecstasy as the blood froze against my frost-encased breast.

The things fought with a rabid ferocity wilder and much more savage than the common vampyre. They were incredibly fast and moved in quick, staggering motions that were difficult to anticipate. Thankfully, I felt more empowered than ever, as something about spilling the blood of this new breed seemed to fill me with a greater amount of strength than usual.

One of the beasts charged at the regal swordsman from behind—who was preoccupied slicing open the chest of another fiend. I launched myself between the two, knocking the thing back with my shield. It arose and sprang at me with fangs glistening. Leaping high, I jumped over the assailant and landed on the ground behind it. As the monster swiped at the air where I previously stood, I released my shield and raised my sword high, gripping the hilt with both hands. I stabbed mightily into its back, piercing between its shoulder blades. Driving the spectral blade downwards, I opened a long, vertical incision which bared its spine. Taking one hand from the sword hilt, I grabbed the monstrosity by its naked spinal cord and lifted it into the air. The hellion writhed and hissed as globs of ichor and gore spilled from the gaping hole in its back. The ghostly frost of my being—that was like poison to vampyres—crawled from my gloved hand into the body of the villain. The thing howled and moaned awfully. With great hatred, I tightened my grip and watched as the Cosmic Ice did its work. I reveled in the might I felt and roared in triumph as black blood gushed out of all the creature's orifices. Its frozen vertebrae shattered and it died before my eyes. The mutilated husk fell to the ground, and I threw the remaining spinal fragments to the tainted earth in disgust.

Turning, ready to face another attack, all I saw before me was the lone stranger standing with his cloak about him, facing me with sword sheathed and arms folded—the corpses of all the remaining creatures scattered in bloody pools on the ground around him. He turned to me and spoke.

"Impressive feat, I must say."

"You did fine work as well," I replied, sheathing my own weapon.

"I've had some experience dealing with these creatures."

"That I can tell. Do you know of their origin?"

"I thought you of all people would be aware of that, Karnov..." The stranger smiled.

I looked at the man questioningly; as I found it odd that he knew my name.

Then I saw them—two pearly white fangs protruding from the crimson lips of his grin shining in the yellow lamplight.

"Fiend!" I cried and drew my sword again. "I knew something wasn't right about you the moment I laid eyes upon you."

"Halt, warrior." The Nosferatu raised his hands. "I mean no harm to you or your kind."

"Nay! You are a vampyre, and therefore you shall die like the rest!"

I lunged at him with my blade, but he leaped aside, quick as lightning, dodging my attack.

"Hearken! I wish to aid you in this struggle..."

I struck again and this time the vampyre drew his blade, parrying the blow.

Thrice more I struck and was blocked each time... Then again... and again...We were now engaged in a one-on-one fencing match—my phantom-clad steel against his antique rapier, which never seemed to falter in its defense. Although my broadsword should have shattered the smaller weapon, somehow it did not. The pale nobleman was a flawless duelist, as he leaped and dodged, evading and parrying my every attack.

"Hear me out, Karnov!"

Obsessed that the vampyre must die, I ignored his every plea.

I swung at his neck in an attempt to decapitate him, and this time his image faded into space and trailed off to the side as my hungry broadsword swiped thin air.

"Devil's trickery!" I shouted in frustration as I turned to where he had morphed and continued hacking away at his parrying blade.

I started to notice that never once did he take an opportunity to strike at me. He was always on the defense and constantly trying to make peace. I thought to myself that this was very much unlike common graveyard vampyres who would normally be hissing and slavering, taking every chance to try and suck my veins, despite my otherworldly appearance. I also thought of how he had sought to save the two drunken youngsters, who would've been an easy meal for any prowling undead.

"Damn you! Listen to what I have to say!" he yelled angrily.

We were nearing an old, wooden selling-booth. I conjured up all my strength and battered his blade, driving him backwards until we were upon the structure. I then took an opportunity and with a massive blow, kicked him square in the chest, knocking him backward. The steel rapier flew from his hand making a loud *klang* on the cobbles. I then lunged forward. With my left hand I grabbed him by the throat and shoved him against the timber stand, pinning him there with the point of my sword against his breast.

"Now speak, fiend!" I said. "For these words you've been yearning to say all this time will be your last..."

The vampyre winced in pain, once again showing his fangs as the cosmic frost-energy of my mailed glove and seething steel was already affecting his undead soul.

He struggled to speak.

"I came here to seek you out... and request your aid, as I too am a pawn in this struggle against the Niaughu..."

"Niaughu? Is that what they're called?"

"Yes, and I am one of the few who know of their secret, as well as the location of their lair. If you wish to banish them from this land you will need my help. The powers of the Cosmic Ice will only aid you so far..."

"But you are a vampyre!" I roared and tightened my grip on his throat, preparing to drive my blade through his heart.

"Yes—but a vampyre of a higher race that means no harm to mankind, and desires vengeance against those who plague this world with evil... vengeance against those who defiled my homeland... against those who slew my family! Does that sound familiar, Karnov?"

I thought hard for a moment, considering this. I hearkened back to the vampyre seductress, Xycanthia—one of the few of their type whom I had held this sort of intelligent conversation with before—and reminded myself that this could well be more damned deception... but never before had I encountered a Nosferatu who spared young men's lives and slew others of his kind. Looking hard into his cold, grey-blue eyes, I could sense honesty, pain, and a longing for absolution. At length, I released him.

The vampyre fell to the ground holding his throat and gasping.

Chapter II
Legacy of the Alunai (Vampyric Nobility Unveiled)

I looked around and saw that the two of us were still alone in the square. Even with all the commotion, no one else had dared to emerge from the Wolf's Bane Inn.

"Who are you?" I asked.

"My name is Asenthine," he said, rising.

"What is it that's so different about you?"

"Allow me to explain so that you understand: I belong to an ancient race of elder vampyres called the Alunai. Our glorious kingdom once lay in the far western land of Seika Heime—amidst the clouds, high on mountain ranges unscalable by men. There we dwelt for ages, reigning supreme amongst the other vampyre nations. Unlike them, we meddled not in the affairs of mankind. With our divine sorcery, we discovered ways to create fine vintages of blood from the Ether, so that we could feed without killing. This allowed us to remain unnoticed and unseen for aeons, honing our magic arts, loving one another, living freely, and creating fantastic inventions of the kind which mortals could only dream of.

"After several centuries, other vampyre kingdoms gained knowledge of us and our great magic—which was more powerful than that of their dark necromantic arts. One such was the evil Cult of Ghormanteia from the Isle of Aschorzotha. Jealous of our superiority, the dark lord sent secret assassins into our domain. They were ordered to seize and capture Magus Garmain Orlock—one of the grand Alunai mages who was the mastermind behind many of our mystical inventions. After severe torture and torment, the mage's eyes were cut out by Nesadomntha, one of Ghormanteia's prime necromancers, and set into two black crystal orbs. They were then sealed with a magical spell, creating the powerful artefacts that you knew as the Eyes of Orlock. Not only did these relics give the vampyre foresight, but he and his wizards also inherited all the sorcerous knowledge of the wizened old mage, which of course, he would use for evil instead of good.

"Using the sacred wisdom he stole from Orlock, Lord Ghormanteia and his newly empowered necromancers were able to summon a whole race of venomous, undead serpent monsters called the Thulagantar, which they harnessed under their control. The creature you slew known as White Wyrm was the last of this race.

"With this foul breed of serpentine devils under his command, Ghormanteia sent the Thulagantar into the mountains of Seika Heime. The creatures invaded and attacked the Alunai within the walls of our peaceful kingdom. Scores of snake monsters slithered through the shining halls wreaking havoc, killing and devouring women, children and men alike, as well as destroying our inventions. We put up a good fight; casting protective spells and hacking the creatures with enchanted weapons. Alas, the Thulagantar were all too powerful, and at length, our kingdom fell to the serpent beasts. That was the end of our reign."

"How did you survive?" I asked.

"Most of our race had been devoured on the spot, but some were exiled to other planes. The Thulagantar's venom has the ability to transport one to other dimensions, as you well know. I on the other hand was one of the most unfortunate who were taken back to Ghormanteia's newly-founded sanctuary—Castle Thornhaven. This, as you also know, was the old Archonea estate which had then recently been taken and desecrated by the Vampyre Lord. Since he and his minions had nearly depleted most of the usable blood that was then present on their native island, they were forced to find a new home."

Asenthine pointed to the mountain ranges in the distance where the deserted castle stood.

"There I was held with a few other Alunai. In Ghormanteia's court we were tortured and used in sadistic games, as he and his dark myrmidons reveled in our misery. We were crucified while zombie vultures nibbled at our flesh, starved for days and then fed liquid disguised as blood that would materialize into a living parasitic fluid inside our bodies, victimized by spells that would cause our souls to be temporarily removed from our bodies and then forced to do battle with the enraged spirits of prehistoric were-apes while we watched—as well as faced with many other treacherous horrors that I dare not speak of…"

"And how did you not perish within those walls?" I interrupted.

"After several years I was able to manage an escape. I had developed a romantic relationship with Noctivia, one of Ghormanteia's favorite concubines. A raven-haired seductress who floated in spectral gowns, attending to the dark lord, she knew much of his obscene wizardry. The vampyress had studied the dark arts since before his time, and secretly knew many things he did not. Each morning Noctivia would enter my chambers covertly after Ghormanteia had retired to his crypt. During these intimate visits, I was slowly able to manipulate her, so that eventually she would answer my every request. The bastard may have taken my magic, but I still retained the clandestine sensual arts of the Alunai, which was unknown to him and his kind. Utilizing this, I was able to induce extreme mental and physical pleasures to his royal blood-wench which she had never experienced before. Doing so ensured her dedication to discreetly answer my every beck and call.

"One day, I convinced Noctivia to cast a glamour of invisibility over me that was effective even to the likes of Ghormanteia and his black wizards. She surreptitiously escorted me out of the castle. Thus, I escaped and fled into the snow-covered mountains, running and hiding in the deep crevices while the daring witch's spell remained effective. Upon discovery of my retreat, I was soon pursued through the mountains by the enraged Lord himself, who rode upon his sled driven by a score of three-headed devil-cats. Even with Nesadomntha by his side and the Eyes of Orlock at his disposal, he was still unable to pierce through the sorcerous invisibility in which I was enshrouded. Never was I discovered."

"If the Alunai's power over women was so profound that you could manage this escape, how is it that no others were able to do the same?" I asked.

"That is because soon after my retreat, the magical barrier was created. Many people believe that the force field Ghormanteia surrounded his castle with was to keep others from venturing in. It wasn't—it was to keep those held within from fleeing. I was the first and only to do so."

I pondered this for a moment.

"An interesting tale," I concluded. "I shall trust that your story is true, since I myself have been in that cursed estate and have witnessed such horrors and witchery as you describe. Now that I know of your origin, pray tell how it is that you are so familiar with mine."

Asenthine's eyes of ancient ice fixed mine in an almost hypnotizing glare. His crimson lips were grimly set, and his pale face was aglow, as the moon had risen higher, now outshining the dimming street light wicks.

"The story does not end thus. After leaving the cursed estate, I journeyed back to Seika Heime with the hope that some of my people may have survived and somehow returned. Alas, the place was desolate. All I found there were crumbling ruins, half-disintegrated skeletons of my loved ones, and the destroyed remains of our once-beautiful magical inventions. I was fortunate enough to reobtain my armor and sword which had been left behind, but that was all.

"Leaving my desecrated home, I roamed the earth disguised as a mortal. I continued to uphold the sacred morals of my race by secretly feeding on the foul blood of game, livestock and forest animals, rather than that of humans in order to sustain myself. Any vampyres I came across during my travels I slew mercilessly, as a great hatred for Ghormanteia and his kind raged rampantly in my heart.

"I spent my days visiting the various kingdoms of man in search of good wizards and magic-users. It was my hope to find one who knew of a way to somehow locate and bring back my Alunai kinfolk who had been exiled to distant realms by the Thulagantar. I soon discovered a coven of powerful monk-clerics hiding away beneath the city streets of Zukatia. They accepted me and invited me to live amongst their ranks. Several of these holy mages claimed to be able to see into other dimensions by means of séance and meditation. I stayed with them for a year, studying and learning much of their arts. Unfortunately, we were unable to locate those I sought; however, my time there was still to my benefit, as some of the magic I had lost was regained by practicing their craft.

"One day, while roaming the bazaars and marketplaces of the city, I saw much commotion and celebration in the streets. Hearkening to two gossiping shopkeepers, I heard them speak of an avenging ice warrior who was said to have destroyed the Vampyre Lord of Castle Thornhaven. As I moved on, more citizens were discussing the same occurrence. People embraced. Some were cheering and waving flags. There was even a lute-playing minstrel on a street corner singing of the 'Triumph of Steel against Fang.' News of your great deed had come to Zukatia, and the people revered you as a savior.

"As pleased as I was to hear of this, I was hesitant to believe it was true. It wasn't until consulting with one of the elder clerics, and seeing in a meditative vision Ghormanteia's severed head at the feet of a knightly warrior in ghostly-swirling armor, that I was able to accept the tale as reality.

"One day soon after this, I was hunting in the swamplands of Karagh-Guhl, not far from Zukatia. While stalking, I was alarmed by a loud, grunting sound, accompanied by a sloshing of water that was heavier and more violent than that which any forest animal would make. Hiding behind a thicket of reeds, I waited and observed. It was one of the Niaughu—the first I'd ever seen. The appearance of the creature piqued my interest. Although it was completely alien in appearance, by the look of its two elongated fangs and blood-dripping mouth, I could tell that it was vampyric in some way. It ran through the black waters of the swamp. Entering deeper water, it swam toward a large mound of earth comprising the north bank. Intrigued, I carefully pursued.

"This mound I speak of was a small mass of earth, fungi, stone and plant matter protruding from the ground near the water's edge. There was a small, black opening like that of a cave mouth. It was here that the monster entered, and keeping a safe distance, I continued to follow.

"The stygian tunnel was hot and humid. There were torches burning along the walls and I could see a pathway of hardened dirt and stone that led downward. This I carefully followed, being sure to remain unnoticed by the dangerous-looking being I pursued. Eventually, I found myself at a precipice. Looking down while hiding behind huge stalagmites that jutted from the floor, I beheld a most surprising and uncanny spectacle. Below, in a large area of the cavern illuminated by orange-glowing brands, was a giant, obscene entity. It was round and appeared to consist of earth, clay, moss, and a multitude of decayed swamp matter. It had long tentacles extending from it and a large tube that was connected to its backside. It had a pinkish face with black, beady eyes, a pig-like snout, and a small mouth displaying short, razor-sharp teeth. This hideous living mass lay writhing in a pool of green slime.

"Many large pods surrounded the thing on all sides. They were tall, oblong and made of a clear, viridescent substance which emanated a glowing radiance of the same hue. Beneath the gelatinous membrane on the outside of each pod was a living creature—same as the green tentacle-headed beast I saw running through the marsh. It occurred to me I had discovered the thing's breeding ground.

"Mounted before the monstrosity and its egg-like encasements was another curious specimen; coming from the ground nearby was a stump-like structure about six feet tall made of a black, fleshy substance. Embedded upon the outside of it were human eyes, noses, hair and lips, all of which quivered and pulsed as if alive. A vertical opening ran down its length which had rows of pointed, yet tubular, fangs inside. Red liquid dripped from this incision and trailed onto the floor. On top of the stump sat a huge flower. It was an orchid—large and grotesque. White with a red spot on each of its great petals that resembled eyes, the flower had a dripping mouth in the center of it that also contained deadly fangs. Horny thorns adorned its stem, and it swayed in the air, hovering above the tentacled abomination.

"I was startled by loud laughter, as a figure in ebon robes holding an arcane staff approached the scene. To my astonishment, it was none other than Nesadomntha, the faithful and all-powerful necromancer-servant of Ghormanteia. None could mistake him, for his long, braided, finger bone-entwined moustache, and the moon-chalice symbol of the dark one's cult tattooed on the side of his round, bald head, marked him as an eternal servant of the slain vampyre lord. Also, at his feet was his beloved pet, Sabarium—a huge vampyric black panther bred by the cannibal wizards of the isle of Iribos. Many nights in thralldom I'd been forced to defend myself against attacks by that cursed beast. I loathed the sound of its demonic purr. Although, seeing the detestable sorcerer again brought the fire of hatred back into my soul, I crouched down even lower behind the stalagmite to further conceal my presence.

"'You are doing well, Esmadrunga,' he addressed the monstrous creature. 'Soon the world will have a new breed of vampyres to contend with. We must overwhelm them in numbers. Continue the spawning!'

"As he raised his staff in the air, two creatures emerged from an area behind him; they were brown, wart-covered humanoids with webbed feet. They had the heads of giant toads. The creatures walked side by side, each holding between them the arm of a dark-haired naked woman who looked to be around thirty years of age. She walked with them as they led, not struggling or resisting, but staggering lazily as if in a drugged trance. Her countenance was pale, and I saw there were two pointed fangs protruding from her lips. She was a vampyre; newly-changed, by the look of the two bleeding puncture wounds on the side of her neck.

"Nesodomntha laughed evilly as the toad-men led the lethargic Nosferatu to the fleshy base of the giant orchid. When they approached, the vertical incision that ran down the foundation opened wider, further revealing its fanged, gurgling chamber. The creatures placed the vampyre inside and quickly moved away. The walls of the thing's orifice immediately snapped shut, crushing her inside and causing blood to spurt out between the small crease of the now-closed incision. The noise of crunching bone could be heard, as well as a sucking and swallowing sound, while the thing devoured the undead woman's body.

"As the strange mound ingested the vampyress, the giant flower attached to it activated. Spreading its leafed extremities, the mutated orchid sprayed purple pollen from its mouth into the air and onto the grotesque being before it. When this dust was breathed in through the pig-snout of the mountainous thing, it sighed and looked dazedly (if that were possible for a creature such as this). Soon afterward, it shuddered and from the pink, tubular shaft attached to its backside, a fresh pod shot out, accompanied by more green slime. It slid across the cave floor and landed to join the others. Within the clear walls of its membrane, I could see the green fetus of another mutant vampyre such as I encountered in the swamp.

"'Yes! Bring forth another!' Nesadomntha roared.

"The toad-men came forth once again carrying a drugged-looking male youth who also appeared to be a newly-changed vampyre. They shoved him into the plant-thing's horrid chamber and the same thing occurred. At this point, I had seen enough and quietly made my retreat out of the cave.

"Returning to the clerics' hideaway beneath the city streets, I learned on that same day there had been attacks in Duros Zuil and Zukatia by these creatures whose breeding ground I had discovered. I told the elder clerics of what I witnessed in the marshland cave. They informed me that the monstrous being I described that was being impregnated by Nesadomntha's orchid was none other than Esmadrunga, the renowned Queen of the Earthly Demonic. I was told she was the life force and sustenance to that entire realm, and must somehow be under the control of the dark wizard. They said that these creatures birthed by the Queen were called the Niaughu, and were a powerful hybrid of the Undead and the Earthly Demonic. When I asked the clerics how they knew of this, they showed me ancient texts depicting drawings of the same entity I witnessed. They explained to me that the Earthly Demonic plays a large role in the cosmic balance holding all magic together, and is a necessary force in the sorcerous world.

"The wise ones also informed me that while I had been gone, by means of meditation and divined hindsight, they had learned much about the cosmic rider who had vanquished Ghormanteia, and that they believed you would be the key to destroying this fiendish new breed of vampyre.

"That night, the clerics helped me enter a deep trance, and I was able to telepathically visit you in your dreams. It was not the purple dedeim which caused your vision, Karnov. It was I who came to you as a veiled wraith, and was able to show you the attacks on this land, and bade you to return…

"And so, my plan was successful, and here the legendary Phantom-Clad Rider stands before me. And so, I ask; after hearing all that I have disclosed, will you, Karnov, who holds the power of the Cosmic Ice, aid me in destroying this evil menace?"

I looked at the exiled vampyre with his regal appearance, and bloodless countenance, standing motionless in intense anticipation of my response.

"Although ye are undead such as those I hunt," I said, "I will make an exception this once and put my trust in you—for I believe your tale. I shall join you, and together we will seek out and destroy the Niaughu as well as this necromancer of Ghormanteia. But know this, Asenthine: if you betray me… if this is some kind of deceptive trap, you will die a painful death by my ghost-hungry blade. Then, to further my vengeance, I will travel the astral planes in search of all the remaining Alunai that still exist in this world. I shall slay them one by one, until your race is wholly extinct, and the souls of your ancestors are damned to haunt my spectral mail for all eternity. This I promise."

Asenthine's eyes flashed. Then he nodded grimly.

"I accept your oath," he said. "And the wrath you speak of I shall not fear, since I give you my word that there will be no treachery on my part. Remember that I risk just as much in trusting you—the only one with the power to destroy my kind with such ease."

"Very well, then," I said. "Now, although I have satisfied my blade's thirst this eve, I still wish to quench my own, and then rest for the remainder of the night. I have journeyed far, and the strength provided by slaying the Niaughu will only sustain me for so long. Would you care to accompany me in the tavern?"

Asenthine looked around nervously.

"Nay," he said. "Although I manage to blend in at times, it is not seemly for me to become too comfortable in a small town such as this. I shall retire to the forest for the night to regain my own strength, and then regroup with you on the morrow. Then we shall proceed to Karagh-Ghul. Until then…"

The vampyre bowed, turned and walked away, as I watched the moon's glare upon his silken onyx mane vanish into the darkness of the street beyond.

Chapter III
Sorcerous Beast's Rebirth (A Feasting of Blood and Souls)

A dreary, gray winter sun greeted me as I stepped out of the Wolf's Bane Inn and onto the street the following morning. I had slept deeply and breakfasted heartily amongst wary townsfolk who regarded me with suspicious eyes. Surveying the scene outside, I noticed that only a few daring merchants had set up shop in the square, and they were heavily armed. The place was much more desolate and somber than usual.

Wrathmane was waiting on the cobblestones nearby. He neighed as I approached and I patted him on the back.

"I hope you rested well," said an unexpected voice.

I turned to see Asenthine's fog-wreathed form standing in the gloomy haze of the square, his blood-red cloak wrapped about him. There was a thin streak of the same hue that ran from the corner of his mouth down to his chin.

"Indeed," I said. "And I see you too have already dined..."

"Yes, forgive me..." said the undead nobleman awkwardly as he wiped the crimson stain from his jaw with his regal garment, leaving a pinkish dew upon his bone-white skin.

"We should soon be on our way," he said, looking up at the hazy sun. "The journey is not far, but the morning wanes."

"Indeed," I said. "Let us be off."

As I donned my helm and prepared Wrathmane, it occurred to me that my companion came with no mount, and thus, would never be able to keep up with me and my faithful steed. Even though we had agreed on a partnership, friend or not—there was no way in Hell I was going to allow a vampyre to ride behind me on my horse.

"You have no horse to ride?" I asked.

"That is a factor which need not trouble either of us, and shall be rectified soon enough," he said, grinning. "Keep a slow pace until we reach Blackstone Vale just beyond yonder hills."

"Very well," I agreed, though not understanding his plan.

We left the town. I rode upon Wrathmane who kept a steady gait while Asenthine walked quickly beside us on the road that led through the dismal farmland I'd travelled through many times. Even though I was a familiar, we still received unwelcoming glances from farmers tending the fields, who spoke not when we hailed.

As the bleak farmstead acreage dwindled off and became a stretch of rolling hills, rather than continuing on into the forest, we broke from the path and veered off to the west slightly. This was in order to enter the vale Asenthine spoke of, which lay on the outskirts of the dreaded woodland.

We neared a cool, running stream at the corner of the valley that ran beneath tall, ancient oak trees just before a meadow. As we trekked along the mossy turf, dreamy memories began to flood my mind, and I started recollecting the many times I had brought my son to this pleasant place on summer afternoons to fish in years past. Sadness and longing once again reigned in my heart, but was soon replaced by a great surge of hatred, and I lusted more than ever to find this disciple of Ghormanteia and flay him alive.

"Halt," said Asenthine softly, interrupting my brooding. He held his hand up and stopped in his tracks.

"Look there…" he said and pointed downstream.

It was a Blackstone Elk—a species known only to these parts. Large, beautiful beasts with thick, blue-black coats and spiraling, gray antlers, they were quite rare, and were often hunted. I myself had only seen one before from a distance as a youngster, and it vanished before I could even get it in my bow-sights. They were glorious creatures, but were said to be quite unruly, and sometimes dangerous. This one was stopping at the water to quench its thirst, and seemed to pay no notice of our coming.

"Stay here and don't make a sound," Asenthine whispered.

I stayed motionless upon Wrathmane and watched as the vampyre silently crept forward in the shadows of the vale toward the drinking animal. Stalking like a wolf, Asenthine came upon it completely unaware. When he neared it, he leaped with uncanny speed upon the back of the beast. The elk bellowed and reared on its hind legs. It swung its head and lunged about, trying to knock the assailant off its back, but Asenthine held on tightly, gripping with his strong legs. When he was able to get ahold of it, he grabbed the writhing animal by the neck. Leaning forward while avoiding its deadly thrashing antlers, Asenthine bared his fangs and bit down into the creature's throat. It roared in pain and bucked even wilder, as blood was drunk from the wound. This went on for a moment, before he withdrew his fangs and leaped off the beast.

The elk swayed on its feet, stumbling forward. It snorted and moaned once before falling to the leafy ground to die next to the bubbling brook. A crimson trail leaked from the wound in its neck and mixed with the flowing crystal water.

Asenthine turned his head and looked at me, panting with blood dripping down his mouth and neck. I shrugged my shoulders, not understanding what the point of this was, or how it was supposed to be beneficial to us. Did he just need to satisfy his vampyric hunger once again?

Then, suddenly—the body of the animal trembled. Its eyes rolled back in its head and it started to convulse. Asenthine took a step back. An uncanny green mist surrounded the creature. It rose slowly and staggered to its feet in quivering motions, animated by some supernatural force. It stood upright and swung its head in whirling motions, hissing and foaming.

Wrathmane stirred nervously beneath me as if longing to attack the thing.

"Easy, friend…"

No sooner had I reassured my horse when I myself started to feel uneasy about the situation. A dark transformation occurred. The mist-shrouded animal writhed and shrieked. Its eyes turned red and glowed demonically like embers from a witch's bonfire. Two shining fangs burst through its gums, extending from its screaming mouth.

Asenthine grinned darkly. It was obvious that he had planned for this to happen, and was pleased with the outcome.

The elk's antlers grew and the dull ends formed into razor-sharp points. It sprang up on its hind legs and shrieked like a banshee, as great leathery black wings like those of a giant bat burst out from its shoulder blades. It roared once again triumphantly and then remained still, standing as if awaiting command.

I regarded the creature with awe. Never before had I witnessed such a transformation, and never had I encountered a vampyre that had the power to change beasts. From all I'd seen and heard, it occurred to me that my companion's ancient race must have been truly remarkable…

Asenthine stepped forward and put his hand upon its muzzle. A low growling that sounded like the purr of an ancient dragon emanated from the elk as the vampyre gently stroked its head.

"I dub thee Merklethenon in honor of the Alunai Princess, Merklannah, who was Goddess of all vampyric animals in times of yore. Now immortalized, in her name ye shall serve our cause—bringing death and destruction to those who once defiled her."

The eldritch beast growled again and lowered its head slowly, as if bowing in allegiance. Asenthine walked beside it and then leaped from the ground onto its back. He looked at me and smiled triumphantly. Although uncertain and wary of his supernatural steed, I sighed and nodded as if in approval.

"Now," said the vampyre nobleman, "let us ride!"

* * *

The sky gave birth to an orange and gold borealis as the sun pierced violently through foreboding clouds in anticipation of an early winter sunset. Its radiance gleamed majestically like blazing fire off Wrathmane's ornate armor, while his hoofs pounded the earth, echoing like drums of Chaos. As fast as the wind, we rode across open plains that bordered funereal woodlands in search of Karagh-Guhl.

Just ahead of me was the Alunai nobleman Asenthine mounted on the back of his winged, black, vampyric elk-steed Merklethenon, whose mighty antlers cut through the air like deadly spears. The crimson eyes of the newly-changed beast glowed eerily through the gloom, and a green mist shrouded him as he galloped forth, fangs protruding from his frothing lips.

Before coming to a thicket that lead into the swamp, Asenthine reached his arm out and pointed a slender finger to the forest that fringed the land to our right. He then steered Merklethenon toward the area he had indicated, and I followed.

Our gallops slowed to a halt and I came up beside him as we entered a winding dirt path in the brooding woods. Orange accents from the setting sun filtered upon the ground through the skeletal boughs above.

"I smell the blood of the innocent," said Asenthine. "If evil-doers be near, then they deserve to die—and if that is the case, than it may be to our great advantage. Remember, I have the power to change humans into vampyres. You need to spill the blood of vampyres in order to activate your powers. It would be wise of us to enter the Karagh-Ghul and the lair of Nesodomntha with your Cosmic energy fully charged. Don't you agree?"

"Indeed," I said. "But you said it wasn't in your nature to drink the blood of humans…"

The Alunai looked down as if ashamed. He then fixed his eyes on mine and his expression quickly changed to that of grim determination.

“I will make an exception this once for our cause,” he replied. “Although frowned upon by my ancestors, I vow that this day, the blood of man is the blood of vengeance!”

He reared Merklethenon, and continued down the crude woodland lane. I followed.

A dense, gray fog permeated the forest, and the howling of timber wolves could be heard in the distance. A drop of blood dripped on my helm and I looked up to behold an old screech owl just emerged from its roost, already dining on an unfortunate rodent.

Asenthine stopped, and signaled for me to halt as well.

“They are just ahead. Look...”

Peering through the dead branches of a fallen locust, I saw in the distance four men standing in an area where the trees thinned a bit. Robed in purple silks and wearing gold amulets around their necks, each had a scabbarded sword at his waist. They were gathered around a crudely made, blood-bedewed, stone altar—upon which lay a naked, young girl, bound, gagged and writhing on the stained slate. Lying on the ground in a pool of blood was the dead body of another young maid who had obviously just been slain upon the altar. To the left of the girl was a shirtless male youth tied to a large stake jutting from the ground. There was straw and kindling piled at his feet and it looked as if the robed men were planning to burn him alive. Nearby were their mounts—four brown mares standing in wait.

One of the men read aloud from a leather-bound tome:

“Great Lord, accept our sacrifice... For, with the blood of these mortals spilled upon this altar, we grant our offering to you...”

Looking closer, I saw the gold amulets they wore bore the insignia of the Cult of Ghormanteia—the same symbol that used to be etched upon the breast of my armour, and the one that I previously used to transport myself to the dark one’s castle. The mark had long since vanished from my mail since his destruction, and an empty space now resided there surrounded by other runes, but seeing it again and realizing these foolish humans were trying to summon the bastard back from the grave enraged me to the fullest extent. I instinctively gripped the reins and was about to surge into the scene.

"Not yet." Sensing my anger, Asenthine put his hand upon my arm, steadying me. "Remember, do not slay until I have changed them."

As the violet-robed man continued to read, another drew his sword and walked over to stand above the squirming girl. He raised the blade in the air and held it over the distressed maid in anticipation of driving it through her heart.

"King of the Undead... rise from thy sleep... A banquet of the most precious flesh we have laid out for thee... Come forth and gorge as this pure body pours its bright vermillion horde about the weltering stone... We summon thee... Lord Ghormanteia!"

As these last words were spoken, Asenthine reared Merklethenon and charged from the forest gloom into the space occupied by the murderers. Before the surprised cult member holding the sword could plunge it through the girl's chest, Asenthine leaped from the back of his vampyric elk and came down upon the man, knocking him to the ground and causing his sword to fly from his grasp. As the fiend struggled to rise, the vampyre held him to the earth. Gripping him by his now exposed shaggy brown hair, he pulled his head back, revealing his naked white neck. Fangs bared, slavering, and looking more ferocious than I had previously witnessed, Asenthine bit down into the man's veins.

One of the men-at-arms attempted to attack the vampyre in order to save his comrade, and received a swift kick to the skull by Merklethenon which knocked him unconscious.

Asenthine lifted his head up from drinking and gasped for air as if emerging from water. Hissing and growling in ecstasy, his reddened mouth dripped with crimson gore, and his eyes were savage with bloodlust. He must've been extremely strong-willed, as I could tell he took just enough blood to cause the transformation, and had to force himself to stop.

Seeing the unconscious man upon the ground, Asenthine arose and moved from his current prey to begin feasting upon the next victim. Merklethenon stood between the vampyre and the remaining cultists, guarding him while he drank. Reluctant to abandon their ritual due to this interference, the man holding the book stepped back and began chanting protective spells. The other armed man lunged forward, attempting to slash the enormous elk with his sword. The vampyric beast avoided the blow by opening his mighty jaws and chomping down into the attacker's arm as he thrusted. Merklethenon thrashed his head once and violently ripped the man's arm from his socket. Blood poured from the wound, dying his purple garment a deep scarlet, and the man fell to his knees howling.

Having his first taste of blood, the elk could not resist; he leaned down, and opening his maw abnormally wide for an animal of his breed, bit down into the side of the crippled man's abdomen, burying his huge fangs into flesh and bone. The man's eyes rolled back and he screamed wildly as Merklethenon greedily devoured his lifeblood. The florid luster of the beast's glowing eyes blazed brighter as he drank, and his black, leathern wings quivered in delight.

Once finished with the unconscious victim, Asenthine was upon his feet and advancing upon the chanting sect affiliate, who didn't have time to finish his incantation. The horrorstruck follower dropped the book and drew his sword to defend himself. The blood-satiated vampyre grinned mirthlessly and withdrew his rapier from its scabbard. He struck once and was parried. The man counter-attacked and a duel of steel-on-steel ensued.

Watching through the trees in anticipation, I saw that while the swordsmen battled and the vampyric elk feasted, the drained bodies of the two fallen cultists were beginning to arise. Moving in weird, staggering motions, the robed figures stood upon their feet, taking their first looks at the world through undead eyes.

This was my signal to move in. I urged Wrathmane and bursting through the thicket, plunged into the fray. One of the newly-risen wraiths was advancing toward the frightened girl bound upon the altar, ready for its first meal. Wrathmane galloped forth, and unsheathing my broadsword, I swung a blurring arc into the neck of the creature. As the blade hit home, the thing's head went flying, and a fine blood mist sprayed the fair skin of the naked girl.

Before the headless body of the slain vampyre could hit the ground, its undead soul was released from the oozing stump where its head used to be. As the whirling ghost-matter soared into my armor like a moth to a flame, I felt a great surge of strength run through my body and soul. The Cosmic Ice was activated. The frozen, spirit-inhabited substance started encasing my entire frame. Wrathmane roared in triumph, also empowered. His eyes illumined azure and a frosty smoke lifted from his nostrils whilst the phantom-energy eerily cascaded throughout his armor.

Another fiend was approaching the male youth tied to the wooden stake. I turned to face it, pulled the reigns, and brought my warhorse down upon the wretch, stomping it into the ground beneath heavy, ice-clad hoofs, breaking almost every bone in its cursed body. I dismounted quickly, and as Wrathmane stepped away, I dropped to one knee and drove my glowing steel through the back of the vampyre's broken body, piercing its black heart with ease and sending its soul to join the other in my armor, rather than to burn in the fires of Hell.

I saw that the body of the third corpse was reanimating as well. Having completely drained it, Merklethenon had since abandoned the bloodless husk, and appeared to be feasting upon the decapitated head of the previously-slain vampire—devouring it like a spring watermelon.

Asenthine and the lead cultist were still feuding, which seemed more like a malicious game to the Alunai. They fought in circles around the altar. The vampyre smiled and laughed jubilantly as he slashed and parried with his antique rapier. Gracefully he whirled and spun, as if taking part in an elegant dance rather than a swordfight. His red cape flowed in the breeze, as did his sleek raven-black mane that framed his pale blood-stained face—now orange, illuminated by the setting sunlight filtering through the trees. He was on the offense as he mercilessly drove the sweating partisan backwards. It was all the struggling man could do to keep his footing.

At last, weary of swordplay, Asenthine slashed his opponent's sword arm, severing the tendon in his wrist and causing him to drop his weapon. He then lunged forward and grasped the disarmed energumen by his throat. He ripped the golden pendant bearing the insignia of Ghormanteia from around the man's neck. Asenthine held it before him and spat upon it.

"Traitor!" the vampyre growled through clenched fangs, his eyes wide, bloodshot and dilated. "If you so love the bastard, perhaps you wish to become like him. For your treachery against all that is good and holy, I vow that this day forth, thou art damned!"

Without hesitation, Asenthine pulled back the cultist's head and bit down into his neck. The man screamed and his eyes rolled back as his blood was drunk.

As I finished slaying the third newly-changed devil, I noticed that Asenthine was taking much longer with this last victim. I knew he had already drunk enough blood to change the man, and was ravaging greedily like a common vampyre. Knowing that this was against the moral code of his ancestors, and that he would not wish for it to occur, but was not in his normal state of mind, I intervened.

"Asenthine, enough!" I said as I ran over and pulled him away from the drained man. He gasped and fell backward upon the ground with crimson ichor gushing from his mouth. I looked at the man's face. His transformation had begun, and he was stirring as a fanged menace. Without hesitation, I raised my blade and with two hands buried it in the chest of the evil monstrosity, absorbing the vampyric life force with glee.

Asenthine was sitting upon the ground recovering from the fit of bloodlust that had possessed him. He was breathing heavily and looking stunned.

"Never let me do this again, Karnov," he said, realizing that he had almost gone too far toward becoming like those he hated.

"The work is done," I said, grabbing his hand and helping him regain his standing. "Come, let us continue with our plan."

With the bloodshed and soul-quenching finished, I approached the restrained youth and cut his bonds. Once free, the lad staggered backwards trembling, obviously fearful of my appearance, and terrified by what he had just witnessed. I walked over to where the mares were tied, untethered the largest, and led it over to the boy. I then reached to the ground and picked up a sword dropped by one of the fallen men. I handed it to him, hilt first.

"Here," I said. "Take this weapon and this steed and carry the lass back to safety. There is a full moon tonight. Stay on the path and you should easily be able to navigate through the woodland. Do you know your way to the nearest town?"

The youth said nothing but stared at me, mouth agape. He then nodded slowly.

Standing near the altar, Asenthine made four quick swipes with the tip of his rapier, severing the girl's bonds. She rose from the stone and fled from him, running and sobbing into the arms of the muscled youth.

I turned and mounted Wrathmane.

"Thank you, warrior," said the lad, finally, as he embraced the girl.

Looking down at him from beneath my helm of glowing spirit-mail, I nodded and said, "Thank the will of one of a proud lineage that saved you this night."

I glanced toward Asenthine who had mounted Merklethenon. The vampyre wiped blood from his mouth and nodded once uncomfortably before beginning to advance ahead.

"And tell all you meet who bear the symbol of these cult-men that their time of death is near. For it is no longer only souls of the undead that need fear the vengeance of Karnov and the wrath of Asenthine!"

With that, I reared my empowered steed and then sped off galloping down through the darkened woods, followed closely by my companion, leaving only trails of blood and the green, otherworldly mist of Merklethenon's essence to linger behind.

Chapter IV
Consumed! (A Subterranean Massacre)

A full moon glowering like an eye of Orlock shone brightly upon the swamps of Karagh-Ghul, making its still waters gleam like shining black glass. Surrounded by tall reeds and aquatic vegetation, we came to the morass at late moonrise and began trudging through its muck and marshes. The further we travelled, the thicker it became, and eventually, we entered waters that rose up to the torsos of our mounts, though they carried us effortlessly through the eerie bog. Illuminated by the ghostly light which clung to my glowing ice-armor, I followed behind Asenthine who lead the way with Merklethenon's demonically-burning red eyes piercing the night like smoldering torchlights.

The air was filled with the sounds of nocturnal creatures, and strange cries were heard in the distance. In the dark waters silhouettes of the large blood-sucking eels that inhabited these swamps emerged and encircled us. Some were ten or twelve feet long and a foot around in diameter. They slithered and swam near our mounts but dared not disturb the sorcerous beasts we rode. Also, awake were the carnivorous plants of the wetlands. Thick stalks that held large, yellow, flowering heads baring sharp teeth sat just above the water like floating lilies. I watched as one suddenly splashed down in the water and returned with a large fish in its jaws that it soon devoured. Most entities of the Earthly Demonic realm were allergic to water, but these weren't. The plants chirped and made imitation calls of beasts and humans alike, hoping to lure one close enough to get a meal. They also avoided us as we passed.

"We are nearing the lair," said Asenthine. "Stay alert. The Niaughu could be about in these parts."

The black swamp deepened, and our mounts were forced to swim in order to hold us above the surface. I could see on the shore in the distance an orange light emanating from something on the land. It was this we were moving toward, and as we came closer, I saw in the moonlight, just as my companion had described, a mound of earth upon the land with a small opening from which the glow came.

Eventually, the water became shallower as we advanced toward the coastline with water and muck dripping from our steeds' bulks. Once on shore, we dismounted before the radiating knoll, and I could feel heat emanating from within.

"Wrathmane and Merklethenon will have to wait outside this time, I am afraid," said Asenthine. He patted his vampyric elk who made a grumbling, purring sound.

"There is one thing we must remember," he said. "It is very important that we do not harm the thing known as Esmadrunga during battle. Doing so may disrupt the Cosmic balance on this plane, therefore causing serious consequences that may hinder all magic. Although hideous, and currently under the control of Nesodomntha, she is still the Queen of the Earthly Demonic, and a necessary entity to this world."

I nodded in agreement, eager to begin the fight.

We entered the stygian hovel with slight difficulty. Asenthine's sleek frame slid through the opening with ease, however, my armored bulk required a bit more force to squeeze through. Eventually, we both dropped through the entrance and onto a hard, earthen floor from which a pathway led downward. The moss- and fungi-covered walls of the cave were tight and elucidated in a dim, golden light issuing from mounted torches, which were fueled by an unknown source. Reptiles, giant insects, and a weird species of white, eight-eyed, centipedal snakes crawled and slithered around as we advanced down the sloping path.

As we descended, the temperature continued to rise. When the lane came to a sharp turn, we saw a figure around the bend in the distance. It was one of the Niaughu. The thing was on its knees and feasting on the blood of a huge swamp rat. Asenthine and I both drew our swords. At the sound of steel being unsheathed, the hideous beast turned its tentacled head toward us and roared. It dropped the rodent, rose to its feet and came rushing at us, ready to dine upon our flesh. As it approached with outstretched claws and elongated fangs, Asenthine slashed it across the chest once with his rapier, and then ducked to dodge and lunge behind it in the close quarters. As it came upon me, I followed the attack by driving my blade deep into the creature's rib cage, piercing its heart. It howled as jade ichor gushed from its body. When the monster collapsed to the floor, its soul came soaring out of its body to join the other vampyric wraiths inhabiting my already gorged armor. As I absorbed it, I felt a great surge of power. The tainted spirit of the Niaughu added even more strength and vitality to that of which I had already acquired by slaying the previous four vampyres in the forest. I sighed in ecstasy as my ghostly aura intensified.

Continuing onward with swords drawn, the warm tunnel descended lower and widened. When nearing a small still water pool, a booming voice was heard in the distance. Approaching what was like a forest of stalagmites, we slid between the stone masses until eventually coming to the edge of a precipice. Hiding behind the pointy structures, we observed below.

It was exactly as Asenthine described; a large, rocky chamber illuminated by orange and green lights. The horrid creature called Esmadrunga was seated amongst a pool of emerald slime on the subterranean floor. The glutinous thing looked like a massive barrow of earth and vegetation. It had a horrid face with writhing tentacles, and resembled a human brain. Small black eyes gazed over an impish pig-snout. Its disgusting mouth was slack-jawed and it drooled lazily as a haze of purple dust lingered in the air around it. Surrounding it were scores of pods containing unborn Niaughu.

Clad in an ebon robe, Nesadomntha stood in the center of the spectacle, his tattooed head and long mustache giving away his identity. At his feet was the vicious black panther, Sabarium, chewing on what appeared to be a human leg bone. Waving an arcane staff, the necromancer noisily commanded two toad-men who ran to and fro bringing naked, lethargic humans from an unseen area of the chasm. Chained to the walls by iron shackles were several vampyres—male and female—dressed in rags, hissing and slavering. The amphibious henchmen led the humans to the vampires, and watched them feast on their blood. Before the creatures drank too much, the humanoids beat them back with silver staves, croaking "Enough." As the bodies were released, the servants carried the newly-changed vampyres to be inserted into the mouth of the orchid-mound. There was no struggle, as they were lethargic, and in the brief state of shock that occurs just at the moment of transformation. By the time they had become active, and gained their Nosferatu senses, they were already being devoured by the heap.

The giant, white orchid sprayed a violet pollen-cloud onto the queen, and as soon as a pod slid out of the tubular shaft attached to her, the toad men were already returning with another victim in their clutches to feed to the hungry mound.

Sickened by this spectacle, I could no longer stand and watch this horror give birth to more mutant entities.

"Let us move in," I said to Asenthine, who nodded and drew his rapier.

We moved along the rocky path leading down through the stalagmites until we came to the chasm floor where all was taking place. Unseen by the preoccupied villains, I made our presence known.

"Halt, fiend!" I yelled.

The salientian servants stopped in their tracks, and Nesadomntha turned with a surprised and enraged look upon his face. Dropping the half-eaten bone, Sabarium sprang to his feet, growling ferociously.

The sorcerer laughed.

"I see we have guests!" he jested. "Indeed I remember this Alunai who escaped our clutches and fled into the mountains, never to be discovered. How nice of you to pay us a visit."

Asenthine scowled and gripped his sword hilt tighter.

"And you, cosmic warrior," said the wizard with an evil gleam in his eyes. "I have not yet had the pleasure of making your acquaintance, although I have heard many things about you. From what I understand, you are the one who is responsible for the destruction of our great Lord. For that you will pay dearly."

"Hearken, warlock," I replied. "It is you who will taste the vengeance of icy steel this night. For your treacheries against mankind you will die a most horrible death, just like your damned master. Prepare to meet your doom!"

I rushed forward, tendrils of glowing soul energy trailing from my radiating armor. Gripping my charged sword and shield handle, I was ready to slay the necromancer at all costs. Asenthine followed close behind.

"Children, come forth!" called Nesadomntha, raising his staff.

Suddenly, the familiar sound of a slavering mob assailed us, as scores of Niaughu came rushing into the chamber from unseen corners and pathways of the cave.

As they ran toward us, I leaped into the air, diving into the herd. Landing feet-first in the mass, the creatures lunged at me, only to draw back scathed as they felt the scourge of my phantom-clad armor. I hacked and slashed heads off of the creatures one by one, causing their green ichor to mix with the similarly-colored ooze that coated the floor. Some tried to grab me from behind and pull me down, or gnaw through my icy encasement with their deadly fangs. All who dared writhed back in pain with frosty smoke coming off their smoldering limbs.

Asenthine was on the outer part of the fray, executing his flawless swordplay skills which were now tested to the extreme. As the Niaughu attacked him in numbers, the regal Alunai struck fast as lightning, and took down many using the honed skill I had previiously witnessed. With surgical precision he stabbed the creatures through their hearts, ending their vampyric existence.

Oily tentacles blinded my vision. I swung into a Niaughu torso, severing it completely in half, and absorbed its soul with delight. I was becoming so powerful that the mob dispersed, and several of the creatures fled from me in panic. I ran after them through the chamber and slew each I caught. Alien guts and brains splattered upon my shield. I gorged on their essence, much like they had previously done to innocent humans, no doubt. I chased them laughing in triumph.

The slaughter continued until most of the Niaughu had either been slain or had fled to another part of the cavern. As the area cleared a little, I peered through the chaos of dying monsters but saw no sign of the necromancer Nesadomntha.

Suddenly, there was a loud roar and I turned to see Asenthine face-to-face with the evil panther Sabarium. The vampyre hissed in rage and showed his fangs. He had his rapier outstretched toward the growling cat and was circling him slowly. The panther lunged and slashed him with deadly claws. It severed deeply into his upper thigh, tearing through his leather breeks and splattering blood upon the stone floor. Asenthine cried out and swiped once with his sword, barely missing the head of the great animal. Sabarium leaped at him with jaws opened wide, but landed on stone ground as Asenthine tumbled out of the way just in time. As the enraged feline's muscular form came flying toward him again, the Alunai whipped twice with his rapier, and with its point, cut the great cat's right eye from its socket. Blood sprayed and the eye fell upon the ground. Sabarium shrieked and Asenthine once again slashed, cutting a long gash across his shoulder blade before the damnable atrocity fled the scene, pouncing away into the cave's depths.

I sliced another creature through the ribcage and pulled its beating heart from its chest. I dashed the foul thing to the ground like rotten fruit before running over to my companion who was tending to his wounded leg.

"Is it bad?" I asked.

"I'll be fine," he replied. "Quickly, let us destroy the unborn ones."

"With pleasure!" I agreed.

The two of us ran toward the space were Esmadrunga and her brood were seated. The stunned queen was even more grotesque up close. I tried my best to avoid coming too close to the tentacled alien-looking mound of wretchedness that drooled lazily, as if drugged by the subtle pollen cloud that still hung in the air.

Asenthine and I both hacked our weapons into the soft outside membrane of the pods surrounding her. A clear-greenish liquid gushed out, coating our armor as we tore through the amniotic walls to get to the Niaughu fetus. The queer things fell out convulsing upon the ground. As they did, we immediately stabbed them through the heart, or decapitated them. The helpless pups were killed with ease as we sallied forth through the nest, slashing open the placenta-like egg sacs and slaying the screeching, underdeveloped vampyres as fast as we could. Some flopped forth like fish out of water, attempting to bite us, but they were too weak to do any harm. I squashed the heads of many with my boot and Asenthine kicked some clean off their fragile shoulders. Others he chopped to pieces with his rapier. Covered in their birth-fluid, I crushed several with my ice-clad shield, and then chopped them to bits. Many died immediately as they came in contact with the cosmic energy that danced along my frame. Souls flew into my armor endlessly as the genocide ensued, and my strength intensified even more, the glowing aura that surrounded me radiating blindingly like a mantle of godly power.

Suddenly, amidst the slaughter, we heard a loud, deep growl like that of a giant demonic frog. Queen Esmadrunga appeared to have awakened from her daze and was now writhing about—apparently enraged at the many deaths of her young. Before I could react, one of her viscid tentacles whipped out and coiled tightly around my torso like a huge python. As I was raised into the air, I struck downward with my sword into the thing that restrained me, but amazingly, even with my strength at its zenith, I could not seem to sever or damage the thick cord. I marveled at this and continued hacking in haste. My efforts were futile as the queen brought me before her, holding me in the air still trapped in the deadly vice of the tentacle.

I could see my reflection in the pits of her beady black eyes that were seated in the strange mass of squirming, fleshy vegetation that composed her being. Her wet pig-nose dripped a purplish liquid that was the same color as the pollen which impregnated her. Sharp, yellow fangs with insects crawling between snarled from her horrible mouth, and a worm-like tongue flicked in the manner of a reptile.

Asenthine watched from below, standing motionless in the pool of dead fetus matter. I knew that he did not want to disrupt the balance by hurting the queen, as he had told me before, and must have felt helpless to save me. I on the other hand was desperate, and as I was held, started swinging my sword in an arc toward the horrid maw of the monstrosity. I was not close enough, however, and these efforts proved to be useless as well.

Esmadrunga's eyes rolled back and she formed her lips in a circular shape around her fanged mouth. She then began sucking, pulling in air that flew into her mouth like great winds. Suddenly, I felt a strange, painful sensation as the ghostly aura flowing through my armor started leaving my body to join with the stream. The suction intensified and I watched in horror as the vampyre ghosts that provided me with strength were stripped from me and inhaled into the queen's mouth. One by one they flew, and with each one I felt my strength wane more and more.

Amongst the noise of the wind, great laughter boomed through the cavern, and glancing down below, I saw that Nesadomntha had once again emerged from his hiding place.

"Yes! Excellent work, Queen of the Earthly Demonic! Take from him that which was once yours. Devour the sustenance that gives him such strength. Then we shall make him pay for his crimes!"

Agonized, I remained helpless in the queen's grasp while my life force was drained. As the final spirits were removed from me, the Cosmic Ice encasing my armor melted and liquefied until it became a swirling blue substance that moved and pulsed as if alive. I roared in agony as it too was stripped from me and sucked forth into the queen's greedy mouth. The glowing aura that surrounded me had vanished and I felt as if all my vitality had gone with it. Esmudrunga licked her lips in ecstasy as she feasted. The alien liquid quivered reluctantly in the air as it was pulled with the windstream. While it was being stolen, I felt as if every bone in my body was breaking.

When the last bit of the cosmic matter was devoured, the tentacle holding me loosened its grip and I was dropped to the cave floor, landing in the splattered guts of the infant Niaughu. The queen relaxed and fell into a deep slumber, seemingly satisfied by the feast. I tried to rise but was too exhausted to move. All my strength—even that of a mere mortal—was utterly depleted.

"Now, children!" cried Nesadomntha. "Return! He can no longer harm you. Come forth and avenge your brothers and sisters!"

From the cavern's depths a scattering was heard. At their master's call, the remaining Niaughu were returning.

Quickly, Asenthine ran over to where I lay. Conjuring all his might, he lifted my limp frame into his arms and tossed me over his left shoulder with strength that seemed uncanny for one of his stature. Carrying my heavy, armored bulk, he ran while the Niaughu chased us. Asenthine sprinted out of the chamber and back onto the path that led upwards. As one of the creatures approached him, he swiped behind with his rapier held in his right hand. The thing's neck was severed. Its head hung by a thread before it fell.

My mind spun and my whole body ached as I lay nearly lifeless in the grasp of my vampyre friend. Whenever I opened my eyes, images were hazy and distorted. I heard only Asenthine's panting, a running mob of creatures, and Nesadomntha's mocking laughter echoing through the bowels of the tunnel below.

Asenthine made his way steadily upward, keeping a safe distance from the pursuing monsters. The clumsy, newly spawned Niaughu were fast, but could not compete with the speed of the vampyre. As he came to the remains of the slain creature we had killed during our descent, he kicked it and caused the body to roll down the path, tripping many of our pursuers and causing the whole mob to stumble. Asenthine hastened, picking up his speed even more. As he came to the opening of the underground tunnel, he stopped, took me in both arms and leaped in a floating manner—as if in flight—out through the overhead cave opening, and onto the swamp bank where our steeds were waiting.

Merklethenon was standing near, but Wrathmane had fallen. Since the Cosmic Ice had been stripped from me, he too, had lost his powers. He appeared to be drained, as I was. Asenthine quickly laid me on the back of the black elk and mounted the beast himself. He then commanded Merklethenon in a tongue I did not understand. Suddenly, with the two of us upon his back, the elk stood over Wrathmane. In an instant his legs began to extend, so that he grew taller. Then, bending his knees unnaturally outwards, he wrapped his elongated limbs around the bulk of the lame warhorse, grasping its body like a spider holds its prey. The moment the slavering Niaughu emerged from the cave, Merklethenon beat his leathery wings and rose into the air carrying Asenthine and I upon his back, with Wrathmane in the grip of his mighty legs. Soaring into the moonlit night sky, the majestic beast bore us away. I looked down once and saw the orange glow emanating from the cave opening. The Niaughu swarmed around the beach like ants, enraged before the black brooding waters, as we rose higher, leaving behind the cursed swamp and its horrors. The chill of the night wind caused me to shiver, and it was not long before I became unconscious.

* * *

I awoke to the sound of crackling flame. Sitting up painfully, I discovered that I had been laid upon a forest floor before a campfire. It was still dark. Wrathmane was also lying on the earth nearby and Merklethenon was standing by him.

My head was pounding, and every muscle in my body ached. I tried to stand and then quickly sat back down, realizing I was too weak. My stomach churned and I vomited upon the leafy ground. Hearing a rustling in a nearby thicket, I reached for my sword which was still at my waist. I relaxed and was relieved once I beheld that it was but my companion Asenthine emerging from the surrounding brush. In the glowing firelight I saw that he was holding something in his hands, and had herbs bandaged around his wounded leg.

"How are you feeling?" he asked in his strange Alunaian accent.

"Like I've been through Hell and back," I replied.

"Drink this."

The vampyre handed me what looked like the bladder of some large animal that he had filled with water. I took it from him and drank. The water was cold and had a faint taste of blood. I guzzled all the contents and breathed deeply.

"Thanks," I said.

Asenthine sat down upon the ground, across the fire before me. The moon gleamed on his straight onyx mane and ebon gauntlets. He had a crimson stain upon his lips that perfectly matched the color of his long cape. It was obvious that he had just feasted.

"You will regain your strength in time," he said. "However, the queen has confiscated your Earthly Demonic sustenance, which is the essence of one of the three combined soul-types that made you what you are—or should I say, 'were'? Now that it has been taken away, you no longer possess the power of the Cosmic Ice."

I looked down at my dull, gray armor. It had lost its ethereal luster, and there were no longer any runes etched upon it. In truth, I looked like nothing more than an ordinary warrior returning from battle. I glanced over at Wrathmane who had also been weakened, since his power was an extension of mine. He lay there, ill-looking, like a lame stallion in a Duros Zuil pasture. I frowned and held my aching head in my hands.

"So, Karnov," said Asenthine. "We have failed to destroy Nesodomntha, and as we speak, more Niaughu are being bred as a weapon against mankind... Now that you—the only one in this world capable of destroying them—have lost your supernatural ability, what do you propose to do?"

I looked up at the sky, and brooded silently for a moment while gazing at the dimming stars. Memories rushed through my mind of all that had transpired since my meeting with Asenthine in the market square. I felt as if a part of my soul had been stolen from me along with my faculties, but my courage and strong will still remained. Most of all, the hatred and the longing for vengeance that reigned in my heart burned brighter than ever. At length, I sighed, looked him in the eye and said:

"I think there is a certain witch we need to see..."

Book II
By Howie K. Bentley

Chapter I
The Oracle

It was the heart of winter, and the gloomy evening waned beneath a dull grey sky. Dusk was approaching when we came to the edge of the forest clearing where sat the witch D'vartha's snow-covered cottage. I raised my hand for Asenthine to rein in Merklethenon, and we came to a stop.

D'vartha's hut had always unsettled me, what with the company of malefic spirits and entities that haunted the place, but what I now saw blasted my sight. The house was covered in strange runes—the like I had never encountered elsewhere—and the runes were painted in blood. The hut looked as though it had been visited by a bloodthirsty vandal who had plenty of fresh corpses to supply him with his paint.

"A great evil is afoot!" I hissed in whisper.

Asenthine nodded his head in agreement. "The cottage drinks the light like a succubus taking her lover."

I had lost the power of the Cosmic Ice, but I still retained, to a small degree, the boon I had once been endowed with regarding the perception of occult forces. I squinted my eyes and saw a grainy mist swirling about the house. What great depths of gramarye was it that D'vartha now explored beneath the thatched roof of that hut?

As I focused upon the witch's vine-clutched abode, a curious figure rounded the corner of the house and shewed itself. A pale little girl—her hair the color of straw—sat astride a hog and rode it around the yard. My keen eyesight observed from afar a face that appeared to have never smiled. She wore a white dress as a child might be buried in. Blood was splattered down the front. I saw her open her red-smeared mouth to speak to the swine, and the fangs of the vampyre shewed. Her alabaster gown—the front dyed brightly with splotches of crimson—was that much more pronounced against the image of the cutty black sow on which she sat. The child's azure gaze appeared as that of one entranced and firmly fixed on Hell and nothing else.

We backed our mounts into the shadows of the trees verging on the forest and watched the child. The hog on which she sat paced the yard and rooted around. It snuffled as though poking through old apple cores. Anon, the child raised her head and sniffed the air like a wild animal as chaunting issued from the latticed windows of D'vartha's abode. The door to the cottage swung open, and the girl rode the pig into the house.

Desperate as Asenthine and I were to remain hidden, we had no vantage to glimpse the interior of the witch's home. I scanned the area and saw no immediate threats from the exterior of the house. I dismounted and tethered Wrathmane to a large oak. Asenthine tethered Merklethenon to an adjacent bole, and we slipped in closer to D'vartha's cottage as the chaunting grew louder. Candlelight reflected on the windows, illuminating the inside of the cottage.

I chanced a glimpse through the window under which we squatted. Figures were gathered about D'vartha's dinner table in a circle. They were a ragtag lot. Even those who weren't clad in the garments of peasants wore clothing that had seen better days. Farmers, mendicants, traders, merchants, and nobility were all represented there—both children and adults. Whatever nefarious power held sway over the clandestine assembly did not discriminate.

The chaunting ceased and the figures joined hands and marched widdershins around the table. Anon, they stopped and moved to either side of the table, forming a path. In the brief opening, I could see a woman's severed head inside a cabalistic circle drawn upon the table. The thing was withered and had bloody runes inscribed onto it. The head opened its eyes and spoke. Though the words were muffled, I could make out its speech. I heard it croak in a sepulchral rasp, "Hearken ye now of better days, listen to my words from beyond the grave. He who would have his greatest wish, must endure the shame of the Vampyre's Kiss."

All eyes then were on a thin young man with dark hair who stepped forward and stopped. After an uncomfortable pause, the head screeched. "Come on, boy! It's not like I am asking you to kiss a goat's ass. What is it you want more than anything?"

The boy stammered, but after a few tries, he managed to choke out, "I am from a poor family, and the others always looked down upon us. I would have riches and the fear and respect of all I encounter."

"Then you shall have it. But first the kiss..." the dead woman's head rasped.

The young man looked upon the abomination, entranced. Then he shuffled forth against his will. I don't doubt that there was some part of him deep inside that screamed in protest of the nefandous act forthcoming. But his will was no longer his own, and whatever it was that possessed him made him shuffle over to the head. His own head he lowered to the abomination and lingered for a time. The lips of the bodiless thing must have locked with his, for I saw him straining as though he resisted. He tried to back away, but his feet might as well have been encased in lead. Anon, his body folded like a drained wineskin and fell to the floor. His head rolled and dead eyes looked in my direction. Looked, but did not see. I ducked under the windowsill but could still hear the voice of the head through the window.

"Take him out and bury him nearby in the forest. When the change is upon him, you will dig him up like the others, as was done with you yourselves. Then he will be one of us. Now, go and do Xycanthia's bidding!"

Asenthine and I quickly hid ourselves away and watched the

procession. Fortunately, the company had moved through an exit from the back of the house and away from us. The vampyre coven carried the boy in a coffin and made for the depths of the forest.

"Xycanthia! Damn! This just gets worse and worse," I growled.

"You mean the vampyre you slew? And you did say you cut off her head?" Asenthine replied.

"Aye, that damned head was what was in there doing all of this. The coven that just left was worshipping the head, and it just killed that boy. Or didn't kill him. I have no doubt he will be back in a few days, though a little longer of tooth than when he left here. Well, I didn't see D'vartha in there with the rest of those imbeciles, and we are going to have to find her."

"Any ideas?"

I went over to Wrathmane and took from my saddlebag a mixture of powdered vervain, garlic, and an assortment of various other herbs mixed into a concoction I refer to as Vampyre's Bane.

"Let's go," I said.

"Into the house?" Asenthine asked.

I nodded. "We had better do it before her coven returns. I brought the bitch to heel before, and I'm going to do it again. It's the only way. We have to find D'vartha. She is the only one who can overcome the spells of the Earthly Demonic."

Silent though we thought we were, slipping through the door of the witch's cottage, the severed head of the vampyress immediately acknowledged our presence. It was sitting upright in a small wooden chest—a handy carrying case—with the lid thrown back.

"Greetings, Slayer. It has been a long time…" the head on the table hissed.

Before she could say another word, I flung a handful of Vampyre's Bane in her withered face and said, "Aye, bitch, I am back."

The severed head of Xycanthia choked and sputtered. With one fist, I grabbed Xycanthia's head by what was left of her once-crimson locks and lifted it from the box. Immediately, I poured most of the sack containing Vampyre's Bane into the box and pushed Xycanthia's head face-down into the mixture. A sibilant hiss like that of a den of vipers arose, and I lifted the thing and began my inquisition.

"Where is D'vartha, you ruddy-mouthed slut?"

"I'll not tell you, you jackanape!" came a sepulchral croak from the decapitated head.

I shoved her withered face back down in the box. She cried out in anguish and pain until I lifted her free and held her at arm's length.

"All right! What is it you wish to know?"

"Where is D'vartha?" I demanded.

"The witch has fled far. Far from her home and far from her mind," she said.

"Do tell, Xycanthia," I prompted her.

"No!" she ejected, like a petulant child.

I threw her into the box and flung a heaping dose of Vampyre's Bane into her face.

"My sister is out of her mind," she choked. "She has delved too far into *The Book of Dead Runes."* After a brief coughing fit, she said, "Remove me from my coffin and wipe away these damnable herbs and I will tell you."

Asenthine found a cloak left behind by one of Xycanthia's followers and handed it to me. "She is stalling for time."

"I know, my good man. They shall soon return," I said as I upheld my end of the bargain and wiped the Vampyre's Bane from Xycanthia's head.

"Who are you, weirdling, who reeks of the vampyre, yet is not one of us?" said Xycanthia.

Ignoring Xycanthia, Asenthine drew his blade and said, "I'll stand watch while you interrogate her." He then stepped outside.

"Now, Xycanthia, my patience wears thin," I said. "So I will ask you once more before I feed what is left of you to flames. If you want to continue on in this miserable, abhorrent state, where did D'vartha go?"

A sickening, demoniacal laugh came from the grey withered face, and her lips moved like writhing grave wyrms. "She has gone to the Plain of Gnathongules to traverse Time itself. She is possessed by the rune, Yr. As I have said, she looked too deeply into the well of knowledge that comprises *The Book of Dead Runes.*"

Xycanthia's head let out a brittle cackle.

"She read too far in the back of the book without heeding the advice in the front of the book. She began tilting the runes. Inverting them. Distorting them. Perverting them!" She flicked her tongue at me and wagged it like a serpent, her cachinnations filling the room. "She dug me up, you know—what is left of me after you murdered me, Karnov!" she screeched.

"I gave her your head assuming she would burn it or destroy it by some sorcerous device—"

"No, Slayer! She had other ideas!" Xycanthia interjected. "She buried what was left of me in her garden of the Earthly Demonic to steep in her sorcery and ferment. Then she dug me up and carved these infernal runes into me to make me her oracle. She wanted me to be her guide to the Plain of Gnathongules. She was already drunk with power and losing her grip on sanity when the Yr rune took possession of her. She fled into the night like a wild animal to wade through the mists of Time itself. Her sole pleasure is to be the corruption of the 'innocent and the holy men.'" These last words lingered as they came from Xycanthia's mouth in disgust.

"Why is D'vartha concerned with the corruption of good men?" I asked.

"Unh!" Xycanthia groaned. "Why has woman always corrupted that which they touch down through the annals of myth, legendry, and history? Power. Power! Do you know nothing of the nature of women—or for that matter, men, Karnov?"

I knew Xycanthia was waxing philosophical to draw my attention away from her coven, soon to return, and I was becoming concerned with Asenthine's prolonged absence when the tall man stuck his head through the door and said, "Ho, Karnov!"

He swung the door wide and displayed two bundles of severed heads in each fist.

"They are all accounted for. Twelve heads!" Asenthine said. He dropped the decapitated heads of Xycanthia's former coven onto the floor.

"And the boy they buried?" I asked.

"I followed them. They didn't have a chance to bury him. After I killed them all, I put him to the sword, as well. His head is there amongst the rest."

Xycanthia's mouth opened like that of a slack-jawed yokel, then closed into a tight frown.

"I'll just take these out and burn them while you finish your conversation with Xycanthia," Asenthine said.

"You were saying, Lady Xycanthia?" I chuckled. "Go right ahead. I have all night."

She closed her eyes and played dead. Her lips were drawn tightly until I asked her if she would like more Vampyre's Bane in the box with her. That was all it took.

The severed head of Xycanthia was indeed a busy oracle for some time.

Chapter II
The Tunnel of Sorrows

D'vartha had ostensibly run off to the Plain of Gnathongules to traverse time in a deadly game of corruption that would manage to open gates to loose forces wild and primeval, chaotic, and beyond good and evil: a potential future that had been here before man, in an alternate reality, but had not yet manifested itself. She was now possessed by a sort of succubus that was not a demon, but worse than a demon—the rune, Yr. Yr was the feminine infernal manifested on our plane of existence.

She had begun by delving into a malevolent tome titled *The Book of Dead Runes.* As D'vartha advanced with her runic experiments, she had come to resurrect her treacherous vampyre sister, Xycanthia, as an oracle to help her navigate the increasingly cryptic passages in the grimoire. Through her delvings in the dangerous practices of the tilted runes, she had descended into madness, finally becoming possessed by the Yr rune, and so had set out in the dark of night for the Plain of Gnathongules to change history and, in so doing, influence the future.

Surprisingly, Xycanthia confessed to us to her own nefandous deeds regarding her seizing the opportunity to restore herself to power. By projecting her black spirit out from her once rotting head—now preserved by D'vartha's lingering sorceries—Xycanthia had bewitched those nearby, anyone lost or wandering deep in the woods. She promised to fulfill their greatest wishes in exchange for a single kiss. Once each had gotten close enough to see the horror they were conversing with, she would mesmerize them and deliver the kiss, sucking out their very life essence and replacing it with her own vampyric seed. Thus the revenants would return from death as her vampyre slaves.

The coven had rapidly multiplied once she had her initial members, for they would steal forth furtively amongst the living and transfer the Vampyre's Kiss where they could. All of this Xycanthia explained to us. So it couldn't have been too long since D'vartha had run off, possessed by the Yr rune. That much of Xycanthia's story I chose to believe for now because I needed to find D'vartha, and it was all I had to go on.

When I put pressure on Xycanthia to restore my connection to the Cosmic Ice, she told me that D'vartha had been careful to instill in her oracular powers that extended to only limited areas of expertise. D'vartha, mistress of the black arts, had craftily blocked Xycanthia in certain arcane ways, the most important to me at the moment being a mastery of the Earthly Demonic. Xycanthia revealed that D'vartha had given her access to certain runes only, denying her too much power, which she might otherwise gain by being able to connect with the complete rune row, and therefore the very realms of creation.

With Xycanthia's head in the chest serving as her coffin, we set out apace from D'vartha's cottage. The witch had agreed reluctantly to guide us to the Plain of Gnathongules and use her oracular powers to navigate the great Menhirs of Time that stood there.

Asenthine and I slept in shifts, guarded as we were against any treachery on Xycanthia's part. The threat of sleeping in a box with Vampyre's Bane choking her certainly did not appeal to Xycanthia, and there were no problems from our wicked oracle—although we well knew that we might as well have been carrying a deadly viper inside that box.

* * *

After many days of travel without incident, we traversed a series of mountain passes until we came to the Tunnel of Sorrows. That is what Xycanthia called it.

I removed Xycanthia's small casket from the panniers fastened to Wrathmane and held the oracle aloft by her hair.

"Brace yourselves, for there will be much remorse, Slayer," Xycanthia's dead grey face told me. "It is likely you will weep, for you will feel guilt for those things you have done wrong in your life, and a sense of failure and loss for what could have been. Even your friend—as highly evolved as he is—may not fare well. It is only for the strongest to bear. Be strong, for I care not to be stranded in the Tunnel of Sorrows. It will be unlikely, if not outright futile, to draw those up here that would take me away and exalt me. Only the weak fall prey to the Vampyre's Kiss, and only the strong and the brave chance to go near the Tunnel of Sorrows."

Xycanthia's dead eyes followed me as I looked at Wrathmane and she said, "It is best to dismount from your beasts. Though impervious to the attacks of the tunnel, your mounts could absorb some of your fears and run off in the... ensuing chaos... if they are in contact with you once it begins.

"Continue straight ahead until you see the light coming through the backside of the cave from the Plain of Gnathongules. It isn't far, but it will seem like endless torment. And it will be at its zenith when you see the light."

I replaced Xycanthia's head in her coffin and shut the lid, returning the oracle to my saddlebag. Asenthine dismounted Merklethenon and, taking him by the reins, the vampyre followed me as I entered the aperture into the tunnel. We needed no torches, for brilliant, blazing jewels of all kinds and colors lined the veins of strata spiraling through the walls of the tunnel and provided more than ample illumination. There was plenty of space for walking alongside our mounts, and I began to doubt Xycanthia's words regarding the nature of the purportedly nefandous portal to the Plain of Gnathongules.

Anon, I heard a stringed instrument. It was the yucixle—the saddest of all plucked instruments. "Did you hear that?" I inquired of Asenthine.

"No. I heard nothing," he said. However, he looked about, his countenance showing concern. I stole a furtive glance at him a second time and was sure he must have perceived something amiss as well.

We hadn't gone but a few more paces when I heard the sound again, and then a female voice singing melancholically in the distance. The head of Xycanthia remained silent. I looked at Asenthine. "Surely you hear it?"

He shook his head. "No."

As the yucixle played, the woman's voice spoke. "Karnov, once phantom-clad rider of the Cosmic Ice. Thou, who hast been cast down, and rightfully so—you were given a great responsibility and you failed. Now your powers are gone." She began to sing, and I was back in Nesodomntha's cave, held fast by Esmadrunga's one tentacle coiled tightly around my torso like a great python. Though I was the strongest I had ever been, no matter how hard I struck with my sword, I could not sever the grip of the abhorrence. My life force quickly ebbed from me. Esmadrunga's eyes rolled back and her lips formed into a circular shape as she sucked in the force that was the Cosmic Ice, draining it from me and taking it into her own being as a sponge drinks water. As the last of the force that was the Cosmic Ice left my form, Esmadrunga's tentacle released me, and I fell lifelessly to the floor.

Asenthine was shaking me as I awoke on the floor of the Tunnel of Sorrows. The mysterious woman's voice trailed off melancholically. "Karnov, you failed. Karnov, you failed." The cadence resolved with an echo.

Whoever she was, she had sung of my battle with the sorcerer Nesodomntha and how the Queen of the Earthly Demonic, Esmadrunga, had vanquished me; and I had gone back to relive it. I was there in that moment again as surely as I now stood in the Tunnel of Sorrows.

Asenthine took in a deep breath and swallowed hard. He seemed to be fighting back something, perhaps something more than concern for me. We nodded to each other, and I said, "Let's continue."

I hadn't been on my feet for very long when I heard the strings of the yucixle again. The woman's voice was humming, and she began singing. What she was singing was now happening to me as the battle with Nesodomntha and Esmadrunga had happened only moments agone.

"Karnov! Karnov!" The voice that was the sweetest sound I had ever heard beckoned me. It was Adaira. My poor Adaira! I heard her singing a threnody over the plucking of the yucixle's strings. "My love has ridden far and away. To save another, but me he'll not save. My love is far, far away. And green grass will grow over my grave."

And there she stood before me with arms outstretched, but each time I moved to embrace her, she receded, falling back and back. Her voice reached me now only ghostlike over the sad arpeggiations of the yucixle's strings. "How could you leave me, Karnov? Leave me and our child while you go to fight a war in a foreign land? Had you been home where you belonged, you could have stopped them. Stopped the vampyre lord from taking our lives."

"I am a warrior," I said. "I fight for those who cannot defend themselves, and I cast evil back into the pit that spawns it! Do not you remember telling me this was why you loved me the night before I rode off to lead Queen Leandra's army against the minions of Suntha Guull?"

I reached for her, and the wind swept her raven locks about her fair countenance; she drew back farther into the mist. She slowly, sadly shook her head and said, "Oh, Karnov. Foolish Karnov." The sword flashed in my hand of its own volition. Before me lay my dead wife and son. "Foolish Karnov. You carried the war home with you. Look what you've done. You have killed me and your only child."

I dropped the bloody sword on the floor and, clutching my head in my hands, I screamed, "No! You had been turned. You both had been turned by the vampyre lord and his legions!" She held our son in her arms. She stroked his hair. He was covered in blood, and it stained the front of her alabaster gown. I saw where my sword had cut her through the neck. Her eyes rolled back and her head tilted slightly. It rolled off her shoulders as she pitched sideways and vanished into the fog that rolled along the floor of the tunnel.

I don't know how long I squatted there with my head buried in my arms, screaming, but I remember Asenthine shaking me and the echoes of my shouts subsiding over the plucking of the yucixle's strings as they, too, faded to naught.

"Get hold of yourself, man," Asenthine growled in his low baritone.

"You heard the yucixle's strings, did you not?" I grabbed him by his shoulders and shook him. Asenthine nodded his head in agreement. "Did you hear her sing the dirge? Did you hear what she said to me?"

He shook his head morosely and looked off. In the throes of madness and my own grief, it did not dawn on me at the time that Asenthine must be hearing voices of his own.

"Come," Asenthine said. "We must get through this. We have to reach the Plain of Gnathongules." Then he shook violently and almost collapsed.

I caught him and steadied him. We made our way through the tunnel. I remembered Xycanthia's warning that the closer we got to the exit, the worse were the lamentations heaped on one's leadened soul by the Tunnel of Sorrows.

This time, instead of yucixle strings, I heard sour notes blown on a number of trumpets. I was a child again of not more than twelve winters. Thon Gjord towered over me, his thick brows furrowed. He clenched his right fist and shoved me with his left hand. It was then that he spied the rock in my hand.

"No rocks!" he said, then added, "We fight fair, rock-picker!"

"That is easy for him to say, standing there shading me like a tree," I thought as the rock left my hand and missed my target. Dissonant notes came from the trumpets again as Thon Gjord sat on my chest and pounded my head into the ground with his meaty fists.

To the cacophony of those horrible horns, a chorus of voices from the children in the village swelled and mocked me as they stood by and watched this missing link beat me into the earth. "Karnov! Karnov! You lost every battle since the first one. Couldn't even protect your wife and child when you got older." The lack of rhythm to their song cradled the awful notes coming from the trumpets as they mocked and jeered me.

It was then that I spake for the benefit of the cruel children, as well as myself. "Well, that's not the way I remember my first fight with the future village idiot," I said through bloody lips that quickly went dry. "I recall him lying on the ground bleeding with a rock beside his head, and I remember him running in the other direction every time he saw me coming from then on." Thon Gjord's head jerked and turned sideways; he listened, quickly stood, and faded into the ether. I got to my feet and shook my head to clear my senses.

Asenthine crouched in the corner of the igneous formation, growling like a wild animal. He tightly gripped Merklethenon's legs as if the vampyric beast was all that remained grounding him to sanity. "No! No, I cannot stop them! They are slaughtering my whole family! No!" he screamed. Only the whites of his eyes shewed in his head. Light from the exit shined brightly.

I lifted my friend to his feet, and he relinquished his hold on Merklethenon. I embraced Asenthine, dragging him into an open sky lit by swirling colors—thick purples like velvet; a bright yellow one could almost taste... like some sort of citrus; greens more pronounced than the most verdant of pastures; and blood red weaving through those, and all the other pigments known to man, and some I had never known existed.

Asenthine fell to one knee. His eyes returning to their normal hue, he looked up at the sky. "Gnathongules?"

I nodded my head in agreement. "I think so." I could hear the head of Xycanthia emanating its terrible hilarities all the way from my saddle bag where her casket was stored. I paid her no heed. My uneasiness brought on by my ordeal in the Tunnel of Sorrows was quickly abating as I breathed in the thin air on the Plain of Gnathongules. I could see it being drawn down from the swirling bright yellow veins in the sky, becoming golden as it permeated the atmosphere around us. It had a refreshing quality that was surely sustenance of a sort, as much as food and drink. A pink mist like swollen clouds spilled all about and rolled along the plain as far as the eye could see. It had a sweet, satisfying taste like the finest of pastries I had eaten in my youth.

I took from my saddlebag the casket containing our oracle and again held up the head of Xycanthia. She startled me by letting out a bark like a great dog, followed by her witchy cackling. It was then that Merklethenon, releasing a long groan that tapered to a pitiful whine, sped away. Asenthine started to give chase, fell to his knees, rose again, and went into a full run after his steed. But Merklethenon spread his massive wings and took to the sky, leaving Asenthine far below. The beast sped away in a northwesterly direction and was soon far out of sight.

I looked Xycanthia in her dead eyes and shouted, "You no-good piece of coffin-lining filth. You have frightened away Merklethenon with your barking and cackling. Infernal fool! Devil's whore! May you kindle the flames eternally in Hell!"

"He he he! Slayer! It was your weirdling friend holding to that beast like a breast-feeding babe to his mother whilst in the grips of his own sorrows and insanity that made his mount fly into the ether, not my doings. I warned the two of you about touching the beasts while under the spell of the Tunnel of Sorrows."

By then Asenthine had returned and heard most of the conversation. He looked at me—his black eyes full of pain—before turning away in shame.

"No matter," the head of Xycanthia resumed. "It won't be a long journey on foot. Look ahead; there are the Menhirs of Time." Her head jerked and nodded as I held it aloft by a strand of hair.

In the distance, I could see the soft pink clouds of fog swirling about the base of a massive crystal monolith—a doorway through time itself. I focused my eyes and saw more of the giant crystal structures as the mist parted and gave way here and there. For the first time since we'd exited the Tunnel of Sorrows, I took Wrathmane by the reins and trudged forward on foot. Asenthine joined me in my trek to the gateways of Time that lay just ahead.

Chapter III
The Gates of Time

The menhirs jutted high into the sky farther than the eye could see and seemed to span several hundred feet of ground. They resembled mountains of transparent ice. Inside the structures ran striations of every color imaginable, like great intertwining veins. Some sort of energy surged and pulsed through the brightly connecting veins. The patterns changed shape and place like cracks of levin cutting through the sky.

"All right, Xycanthia, which one, and how do we enter? And if you try to trick me, just think about a snootful of Vampyre's Bane for a while."

Her severed head growled at me. "Hold, Slayer, and let me reach into Mimir's well with the runes D'vartha carved into my head. The savage witch!"

Xycanthia closed her dead eyes for a time, and then she began humming. Of a sudden, her eyelids popped open and she choked out, "This one. Take this one."

I took Wrathmane by the reins, still carrying Xycanthia's head in my other hand like a bucket. I walked forward a few paces, Asenthine following. I halted in front of the monolith and asked of the oracle, "How?"

"Just walk into the damned thing. Go!" Xycanthia growled.

Wary of Xycanthia's trickery—I had experienced it in the past when she was a whole woman, and not just a head—I looked at Asenthine. He nodded, reassuring me. We really did not have any choice at this point but to trust the devious oracle. I led Wrathmane into the base of the crystalline structure and felt myself ascending as I walked, although there was no effort of climbing.

The sky undulated with black clouds. Everything was dim, and fire leapt skyward at random intervals. Before us was a great pool of amorphous slime, sentient and endless. The thing belched forth life from its noxious vapors. Reptilian amoebae crawled up onto the small stretch of land that led to the beginning of all things that would be—the archetypes of life itself. Some of the things made their way onto the beach and ran, disappeared beyond the small tracks of land where fire jumped at random intervals. Some of them, more reptilian and well formed, took to the skies on crudely formed scaly wings, screaming horrible cries at being born through the eternally benighted welkin. There were others that barely made it to shore before they were dragged back into the pool to be reformed into only the gods of the pit know what. I looked behind me, but it was as if Wrathmane, Asenthine, and I had never passed through the door from the massive menhir that had let into this world. The headless thing without organs and limbs that had created life now surrounded us on all sides, save for small tracks of land here and there where fire leapt and licked the All-Night long before man had been the dream of the sea of madness that lay before us.

I held the severed head of Xycanthia before me at eye level, and it let out a high-pitched witchy cackle.

"Get us out of here now, you half-rotten head of a wicked crimson whore," I roared.

"I obviously made an error in judgment," Xycanthia rasped.

"It is not the first time," I replied.

"Turn, Slayer."

"Which way?" I replied.

"The way we came in," the oracle said.

I spun in the direction opposite the yeasty sea that lay ahead of us. We were standing on a small strip of beach beyond which lay the abomination-spawning primal slime.

From Xycanthia's severed head came the eerie sounds of forbidden runes. Anon, a door opened in the fabric of Time. I saw Time ripple like heat escaping a flame. The benighted sky rumbled, and levin licked back and forth across the portal.

"Through the gateway, quickly," Xycanthia croaked.

I mounted Wrathmane and held out my hand to Asenthine. The vampyre returned my grip, settling in behind me to ride pillion. My boots raked Wrathmane's ribs, and the mighty steed leapt from the strip of land where fire exploded randomly on all sides. Wrathmane's hooves touched solid earth, and we were again on the Plain of Gnathongules. The sky above pulsed with all the colors of the spectrum. I turned my horse around to see that the vile and chaotic sea that had vomited forth creation was replaced by the colossal structure wherein the genesis of all things was now contained, one of many massive monoliths on the Plain of Gnathongules.

I held up the head of Xycanthia and shook it with anger. "Try again, crimson succubus! And this time, don't lead us astray, or it will mean your end."

"A mere setback, Slayer! I assure you I meant no deceit," Xycanthia pleaded. "I am—after all—but a poor severed head working with tilted runes—and not a full set, at that, I might add."

In a hushed voice, I consulted Asenthine, who now sat behind me.

He whispered in kind, "I fear we have no other options at this point, Karnov." And after a brief conversation with the vampyre, I agreed not to dismount from my horse and burn Xycanthia's head on the Plain of Gnathongules, although at that moment, I sorely wished to do it.

Here I was in a jam I would have never predicted: stuck in limbo between intervals of Time, with a vampyre riding on the back of my horse and taking directions from a treacherous severed head—returned from Hell—who could at any moment leave me stranded in the past, present, or future.

As far as Asenthine was concerned, I liked him and was beginning to trust the vampyre as much as one can trust another formed of flesh, for it had been my way in life to trust only steel when it came right down to it.

I held the head of Xycanthia in one hand and the reins to my mount in the other as we sauntered along the plain, passing and weaving through the many crystal menhirs that reached high into the kaleidoscopic sky. The pink fog rolled along the ground and covered the bases of the colossal structures. Xycanthia chaunted constantly, weaving the bind-runes that would unlock the mystery as to the whereabouts of D'vartha, mistress of the black arts.

Anon, the severed head danced in my hand excitedly and reverted back to speaking the language I know. "This one!" Xycanthia hissed. "Here is the doorway!" Again she chaunted in a language unintelligible to me and quickly vibrated a complex series of vowels and consonants.

"Quickly, Slayer! Herein lies the world where D'vartha now resides!"

Chapter IV
The Knight of Darkling Reich

With booted heels I prompted Wrathmane, and he leapt through the shimmering portal Xycanthia had opened with her gramarye. Into the great menhir we sped like a missile shot from a trebuchet. Anon, we were atop a mountain under a bleak autumn sky. I could almost taste the sweet alpine air as Wrathmane carried us down to the world below. For hours it seemed we wound through miles of narrow passages where basalt cliffs jutted out like charging knights, where one slip of my horse's hooves could have led to a quick, plummeting death far below. Eventually, we reached level ground and traversed a great distance through dimly lit fungoid forests. There my nostrils were assailed by the familiar scent of rotting wood. The world we found ourselves in reminded me of many lands I had travelled in my own world and time.

"Karnov, halt!" Asenthine ejected. I reigned in my mount and listened. "Do you hear it?" he said.

I nodded. "I do now." Screaming; horses whinnying; the clashing of steel on steel; the rustle of chain mail—all too familiar sounds. The stench of wound dew wafted forth on the wind. "Many men have died, and some are still dying!"

Slowly, I ambled Wrathmane forward along the path that exited the forest just ahead. In that clearing on the edge of the forest, one shiny, solid black figure battled many. All about the field were strewn corpses shorn of limbs. Shattered helmets lay beside bloody faces. Upturned beards showed beneath them slit throats where fresh blood still flowed. Bodies lay still, shot full of protruding arrows. Rent mail and shattered breast plates were in abundance. It was obvious that two armies had clashed and one had all died but for a single man. Of the force opposing the lone figure, only a handful now remained.

I unsheathed my sword. "Six against one!" I growled and

charged into the fray. Asenthine followed, and Xycanthia's head swung like a pendulum from my saddle, her horrible cachinnations filling the air.

Before I could reach the knight's side, he slit one man's throat with the point of his sword and clove another fighter from neck to breastbone with the return stroke. Spinning his sword backwards, he stabbed a stealthy attacker through the chest with an overhand thrust. He used his other hand like a hammer on the base of the pommel, and blood gushed from the man's mouth onto his silver breast plate.

Asenthine and I were now on the remaining three. I slashed with grim delight, and the heads of the two remaining soldiers sailed through the air. Asenthine's rapier pierced the third man's heart quickly and withdrew. The knight's assassin headed over onto the ground.

The last living man in the battle of two armies stood before us in silence and leaned on his great black broadsword. Drenched in blood though the blade was, I could see runes etched along the length of the glaive.

The figure was encased in some sort of black steel that looked more like polished obsidian than any metal I had known. His shiny black suit of armor was spackled from visor to metallic-shod heel in blood. And from the looks of his present state of health, most of it was not his own.

"Greetings, noble knight! You have fought long and valiantly," I said as I gazed at the corpse-strewn battlefield. "It appears you are the lone survivor of the two clashing factions. Might I ask your name, and from where you hail?"

He stood there as still as an image of stone. Thinking that maybe he did not understand me, I started to rephrase my question when he interrupted me. Without raising the visor of his shiny black basinet, his voice rumbled sonorously. "One army!"

"One army?" I said.

“One army. They all came against me. I leave a feast for the wheeling kites, and tonight their widows wail. What business is this of yours?”

“We seek the witch D’vartha. Maybe you know of her? She has long red hair and piercing green—”

The knight’s head jerked as if he were a dog being called by his master. He listened for something that neither I nor Asenthine could hear, perhaps a voice from beyond… I knew not what.

Suddenly the knight was upon me. I barely blocked his broadsword in time as he brought it down upon my glaive like a mighty butcher’s cleaver. Asenthine was by my side, his rapier whistling through empty air where the ebon-clad knight had just stood. I leapt to my nemesis and delivered a blow that should have shorn helmed head from shoulders, but the knight easily blocked my blade. For the brief interim that my steel contacted his, I dug my heels into the earth and pressed two-handed against his blade. With a shove that seemed effortless, he drove me to the earth, flat on my back.

Asenthine was behind him, thrusting his rapier. The knight spun, knocked the vampyre’s blade from his hand, and slashed a killing blow as he brought his broadsword around to split Asenthine’s head open. If it weren’t for his quick vampyric reflexes, Asenthine would have been destroyed. As it was, he still sustained a blow to the head and fell to the ground.

I was on my feet, sword in one hand, dagger in the other. I brought my glaive around. The knight leaned back to dodge the blow; when he did, I stepped in and thrust upward with the dagger. With the flat of his sword he knocked me to the ground, and his steel-shod foot came down upon my hand and broke the grip on my dagger. With a one-handed slash, he knocked my sword from my hand. As he raised his mighty broadsword above me two-handed and prepared for the quietus, I heard the rumble of horses’ hooves. He turned to face the charge coming over the verdant hill toward us. Again, I noticed him cock his head as if he were listening to something far away, something, it seemed, out of range of the battlefield.

I got to my feet, but before I could reach my sword, an armored white stallion came charging riderless into the clearing, and the black knight had sheathed his sword, leapt onto the charging mount, and ridden out of sight before the approaching horsemen could reach us. Asenthine meanwhile had regained his feet, but a gash dripped crimson across his forehead and ran in rivulets down into his strange eyes.

* * *

The Abbot Eothoclemes' grey-bearded face was kind but solemn. He sat straight in the sturdy, high-backed chair opposite us, fumbling at his robes of emerald and nacarat. His brow was furrowed beneath his close-cropped white hair and low forehead. The wizened old monk looked every inch the philosopher.

"The two of you are lucky to be alive," Eothoclemes said, nodding to Asenthine where he sat, somber of countenance.

The vampyre's powers of regeneration had healed his head wound considerably, but there was a pucker in his forehead, and it jutted out slightly where the wound was still closing.

"I have never met such a formidable foe in battle," I said.

The old man nodded in agreement.

"Who is this man that can vanquish a whole army by himself?" I asked.

"He is the Knight of Darkling Reich," Eothoclemes answered.

"What is Darkling Reich?" I said.

"It is a shifting demesne of darkness and death," the abbot said.

"Shifting?" I asked.

"Yes. When the knight first appeared, he slayed a number of

Count Debrackle's men. A band of hand-picked soldiers—Debrackle's best—left here and followed him after he had kidnapped a woman staying at the castle. At the time, the knight's dark demesne was seen on Allington Plain. It has since moved three times. It was last seen on the other end of Karava Forest a few miles from where Debrackle's army had ridden upon you and your friend doing battle with the knight."

"It wasn't much of a battle, I'm afraid. Had the count's men not ridden along when they did…"

Eothoclemes closed his eyes, understanding. "How did the two of you come upon the knight's works of carnage?" he asked.

"It is a rather long story, but I will sum it up as succinctly as I can, and then if you would be so kind, I need to inquire of you regarding a matter that is very urgent, and the reason we came here to begin with."

"Certainly," the abbot said.

"Guided by a strange oracle, Asenthine and I traversed the Plains of Gnathongules to find a doorway through Time so that we might seek the witch D'vartha. We were told by said oracle that the woman is here in your world and that she is fey and ran off in the middle of the night."

Eothoclemes stiffened in his chair, his blue eyes fixed intently on me. "Is this fey woman of whom you speak a red-haired wench with green eyes like a cat that shine with madness as though a demon resides within her?"

"Aye. I am told that she is possessed now. We came here to take her back to our world. If she has caused any trouble, we will—"

"Caused any trouble? My good man! We have had nothing but trouble since that one arrived. She appeared here in the middle of the night and cast a glamour on Debrackle. The poor man hasn't had his wits about him since he laid eyes on her. He still sees her everywhere he looks. Word has it he has even been seen rutting with the barn animals, such is the glamour that still lingers here.

The whole castle is gone insane. The kitchen maids were caught cooking human flesh. A few of their husbands have gone missing, so draw your conclusions. Debrackle's castle has descended into madness because of this woman and her black witchery."

"Where is she now, Abbot? I must see her at once. Is she there in the castle?" I asked.

"No. With much pressure from our holy order, Count Debrackle had agreed that she be confined to a room on the west wing of the castle to undergo an exorcism, but she is now gone. Debrackle has taken to his bed and won't move. He says he is dying. Some days ago, I sent a letter summoning Hegumen Hordane the Hierophant. The hierophant is the head of our most holy Order of the Divine Goddess Mirkrash. We anticipate his arrival on the morrow in response to our request for exorcism to remove the malevolent force from the woman.

"I myself had attempted a number of litanies and psalms, but I am sorry to say that all efforts on my part have amounted to only a failed extraction. A strange entity, unlike any I have encountered. The manifestation of a runic force that is feminine and destructive in nature. I thought I had made some progress; things were settling down in the castle. Anon, all changed drastically for the worse one day. I entered her chambers to recite the litanies of Mirkrash. Objects were moving about the room seemingly of their own volition and hurled violently in my direction amidst a barrage of curses and obscenities spewing forth from the woman. It was then that the knight arrived and took her. He rode in on his great white steed and slew man after man, then rode away with her on the back of his mount. I believe the knight is a dark runic force that wears a strange hard suit of shining jet like a man. I believe the witch summoned the knight to rescue her from exorcism, although Count Debrackle believes otherwise."

"What does Debrackle believe?" I asked.

"Debrackle believes she loves him. He believes she was kidnapped by the knight, and he hurls host after host against the knight, chasing his dark demesne through the countryside, hoping to reclaim his damsel in distress. Such is the glamour cast over his eyes that he cannot see his kingdom fallen to ruin and the wholesale slaughter and ultimate destruction of his army. D'vartha's insanity has been… quite infectious."

I finished telling Eothoclemes of our quest to find D'vartha so that he would understand the urgency of our plight.

"What you have told me is fantastic," he said. "But I am not such a fool as to doubt that there are worlds beyond this one, much like our own. There are worlds superimposed on top of worlds. And I understand the severity of your situation, but I am afraid that nothing can be done until the hierophant arrives on the morrow. Although I am erudite regarding dark forces, the hierophant has explored the benighted abysses of the arcane much deeper than has anyone else in these lands."

I cast an alarming glance at Asenthine, and I could tell by his expression that he shared my thoughts. The Abbot Eothoclemes caught what passed between the two of us and spoke. "It is our belief in the Divine Order of the Goddess Mirkrash that one must first explore the darkness to be exalted in light. This means exploring both the pleasures of the flesh as well as spiritual darkness through the black arts."

Asenthine and I nodded our understanding, and the abbot replied with a faint smile and closed eyes.

"And now, if the two of you would care to imbibe some of our excellent spiced wine, you are welcome to do so. We brew it ourselves here at the monastery, as well as our own ale," Abbot Eothoclemes said. He called out to the kitchener, and a man in his early twenties appeared in a plain brown robe with ornate turquoise amphorae and goblets of stone, into which he poured the ruby wine. The abbot ordered food for us, and Asenthine sat in silence as I greedily scarfed down roast duck, boiled potatoes, and freshly baked bread. I realized that I hadn't eaten in days and was famished. I hoped, however, that Asenthine wasn't, because that could mean trouble. But I did not linger on this thought (and no one was reported missing the next day). Thus far, the vampyre had proven himself an honorable and noble companion.

After I had eaten, Abbot Eothoclemes showed Asenthine and me to our sleeping quarters, and they were more than satisfactory for a monastery. On the morrow, we would meet with Hegumen Hordane the Hierophant in hopes that he could help us rescue D'vartha. Until then, there was nothing to do but wait and sleep.

Chapter V
The Hierophant

Hegumen Hordane the Hierophant sat the high-backed oak chair as regal as any emperor had ever sat his throne. Upon his head was the tall miter-shaped headdress proclaiming his office. "The exorcism itself will not be as difficult as one might think." The sleeve to his ornate robe of azure and vermillion billowed as he smoothly gestured with his left hand. In his right fist, he gripped an ebon staff. Topaz, beryl, diamonds, and chrysolite gleamed and twinkled along the length of the haft. On the top of the staff, the claw of a wyvern gripped a large chunk of green luminescence that flashed and ebbed in the dimly lit chamber. Asenthine, the abbot, and I were seated in chairs opposite the hierophant.

"I would hear all regarding the woman's possession from the mouth of the oracle of which you speak." The hierophant's baritone voice rang sonorously throughout the small secret chamber where we now held assembly.

Asenthine proffered the casket wherein Xycanthia's severed head was immured, and I opened the lid and brought forth the hideous abomination. "Have a care. She is as dangerous as an asp in the dark. It usually takes a dunk or two in Vampyre's Bane to procure her cooperation," I said.

The hierophant nodded and studied the shriveled, rune-carved head of Xycanthia as it let out a loud cackle and danced of its own volition where I held it aloft by a strand of its crimson locks.

The hierophant's billowing sleeve flowed as his left hand waved a legerdemain in the direction of the oracle, and his staff rocked deosil in circles where he held it at his side.

"Now, Oracle. I would hear of your part in D'vartha's wyrd," his baritone voice boomed.

Xycanthia's dead eyes closed as if she had fallen asleep, and she spake calmly in the voice of a dreamer longing to return to the land of the dead.

"Karnov killed me. He struck my head from my body and gave it to my sister, D'vartha. D'vartha, the witch. She thirsted for black knowledge as I thirsted for blood and the suffering of those around me. She buried my head in her eldritch garden outside her cottage wherein she called upon the Earthly Demonic... called upon the Earthly Demonic more and more." Xycanthia sounded as weak and faltering as the nails of someone buried alive, scratching at the inside of a coffin lid.

The phosphorescence gripped in the claw at the top of the hierophant's staff glowed scintillantly, and he said softly, "Continue."

Xycanthia's head resumed the tale. "She had obtained a copy of *The Book of Dead Runes*. She said she obtained it from the author and rune incarnate, Thorn himself, though when I looked into Hagal, the world crystal, I could not see all. With a spell of binding, she limited the information I was privy to. I was only her slave, but I still had some wiles about me and tricked her."

"I knew it," I said.

The hierophant held up his hand to silence me and bade Xycanthia continue.

"I told her that a great event would occur. There was an alignment of planets in another dimension that would be presaged by a blazing orb that would pass our world. I told her that she must hurry to take advantage of it. She believed that she had me completely enspelled as her oracle, and she did not study the first part of the grimoire as thoroughly as she should have. I told her there was a short path to the mastery of the runes that lay in darkness. I compared it to the Qlippothic powers of other, weaker systems, so she would understand and believe that I had plumbed the depths of gramarye and returned with the gems of knowledge she needed to master *The Book of Dead Runes* before the great convergence that I alluded to was to come. She called on the tilted runes before she had taken... ah... precautions..."

The oracle fell silent. The hierophant cast another legerdemain and rocked his staff in a circle again. Xycanthia continued. "The shadow of the Yr rune's realm, which is also named Yr, took possession of D'vartha—Yr being the feminine demonic in the heart of the very realms of creation."

Hegumen Hordane the Hierophant nodded in comprehension and as a gesture for Xycanthia to continue.

"D'vartha's descent into madness was swift and terrible. I, of course, encouraged it as I had my own agenda, even from beyond the grave."

"And what was that agenda?" the hierophant asked.

"With D'vartha gone, I would build a coven of followers to exalt me. I, in turn, would feed upon the cult's energy and instruct them in my own art to resurrect me in the body of a pretty young thing that would ascend to a throne, where I would rule as their queen for one thousand years. Perchance a thousand thousand years."

"And D'vartha's agenda?" asked the hierophant.

"Driven mad by the husk of the Yr rune, which I told you is its… her shadow, D'vartha ran off to the Plain of Gnathongules. I told her of the place… the place where she could step back in time, work her way back to the beginning, where all of the myths about the fall of man originate with a woman, there to corrupt man in his holiest and drag him down into the unclean mire wherein sits upon the throne the very incarnation of the fall of man.

"As D'vartha entered the plain of Gnathongules, her intellect and reason became as that of a wild beast. She is powerful and seeks the final fall of man, whereupon he shall not rise again," Xycanthia croaked.

With a wave of his hand, the hierophant tapped the bottom of his staff on the floor, and Xycanthia's eyes fluttered open, then closed again.

My own eyes met the hierophant's cerulean gaze as he spoke. "In our order, the exploration of the darkness within ourselves is encouraged, even mandatory, as to find the light, one must first traverse the darkness. I am from the Northlands. The priests of Wuotan there are masters of the runes. *The Book of Dead Runes* is not unfamiliar to me. Neither is the bouleversement of the rune row and its gramarye, the tilted runes, as Xycanthia called them. By your swords," he nodded to me and Asenthine, "and my staff, we shall vanquish this malignity that has invaded our world and exorcise your friend."

A messenger was let into the room and, gasping for breath, hastily ejected, "Count Debrackle has died in his bed only moments agone!"

"We must make haste and leave for Darkling Reich immediately," said the hierophant.

Chapter VI
Lost in Darkling Reich

Having traversed the pathway through the Korava forest, Abbot Eothoclemes threw up his hand, signaling us to stop. Asenthine and I, along with Hegumen Hordane the Hierophant and a band of the newly deceased Count Debrackle's most formidable swordsmen and archers, reined in our mounts. As we surveyed the eldritch expanse that lay beyond, the abbot spake. "None of this was here previously. Verily, Darkling Reich looms nigh."

With a bow of his head, the hierophant gestured for us to move forward as he took the lead on his piebald roan. The phosphorescent orb atop his staff flared and glowed. The sky turned wine dark, and under its dim radiance, we traversed a sinuous path past scintillating dolomitic pillars of abalone, green, pink, black, orange, and red. We rode past Irminsuls with faces in their bellies twisted and frozen in the throes of pain and suffering. The air became colder the farther we went. And off to either side of us jutted up from the gelid earth the colossal rib cages and skulls of atavisms that had ruled their demesne long before man the beast had ever strode forth. On we rode, past shining caves of gold and silver, wherefrom issued beckoning calls like sirens pining for the death of wayward sailors. The hierophant told us to cover our ears until we were out of hearing range or we would surely go mad.

Anon, we came to a great chasm wherefrom gelid fog rose and obscured what lay below. The hierophant closed his eyes and bade us wait. There we sat in silence, and the wine dark sky was extinguished and left us in utter darkness. Before we could light our torches, an argent orb rose from the abyss and cried silver tears of glistening molten metal. The silvery moon shewed a lake that filled the abyss to the brim and sank into the watery depths. The hierophant rode his mount into the cold lake. We sauntered our mounts in line behind him and entered the waters that led I knew not where.

No sooner had I led Wrathmane into the abyssal waters than I felt myself sinking, and yet I breathed air, and my mount's hooves strode solid ground. An alleyway opened into a deserted street before us. The silvery moon loomed low and ominous before us, illuminating the city and its bizarre alien architecture. It receded, drawing us forward, and we ever followed the shining metallic orb.

The buildings shewed an eldritch geometry that cast me into a drunken stupor to look upon. With but a glance, visions and voices assailed me to where I thought myself in the throes of the euphoria induced by the purple dedeim. I quickly looked away and fixed my gaze on the road that lay ahead as I heard the hierophant urge the others of our band to do the same.

Of a sudden, I heard far behind a rattling threnody such as a roomful of wind chimes might make. I turned to see a horde of skeletons formed of crystal with burning crimson eyes set back in semiopaque skulls crowned by gold and silver horned casques. They brandished sword and buckler and had stealthily slit the throats of those soldiers bringing up the rear. More crystal skeletons burst from the ground.

Those men who rode in advance of the dead soldiers had by now turned and loosed a fusillade upon the crystal warriors. The arrows sounded musical notes where they found purchase. Some of the skeletons fell to the ground, but they quickly found their feet and paced forward to meet us. I drew my broadsword, and Asenthine produced his rapier. We raced to join the other men who were by now engaging the assassins with their swords. Glaives sundered crystalline limbs, and translucent skulls toppled from necks, but on the things fought, dragging down the horses and stabbing into flesh, piercing vital organs and leaving many of Debrackle's men choking on the frothing crimson that gushed from their mouths.

I slashed and parried, slashed again, and a skeleton warrior's head went rolling. I turned aside a thrust as still the thing came at me. I kicked the skeleton from where I sat my steed and it fell, ribcage separating from its hips and rolling on the ground.

I saw Asenthine thrust his rapier into one of the skeleton's jeweled eyes, then another. The vampyre maneuvered his mount (one given him by the abbey) out of the skeleton's path and it walked blindly in circles, slashing and hacking at empty air. I had noticed some moments agone a chaunting growing to the rear of us; then I heard the hierophant shout, "Out of the way!" The hooves of his piebald roan drummed the earth as he came charging in, his robes of azure and vermillion billowing like bat wings. His staff burned a phosphorescent arc and whipped around to strike a crystalline skeleton that had just driven a sword through a soldier. A stream of crimson painted the air, followed by the glowing green that swung around and sizzled on the semiopaque skull of the assassin. The skeleton dropped.

The hierophant dismounted and drove the haft of his staff into the ground. The atmosphere exploded with a dazzling effulgence. I was momentarily blinded. When my sight returned, all the skeleton men lay inanimate. I hesitate to say "dead" because I was never sure they were truly alive. But as we know a man dies, so had the crystal skeletons, for they never rose to harry us again. As I gazed about I saw all Debrackle's men but one lying dead, despatched to the House of Shades by the blades of the crystalline warriors. I myself, Asenthine, the abbot, and the hierophant were all that remained, along with one lone bowman, hight Abnon.

Plunging my broadsword into its scabbard, I drew in a deep breath and expelled it as just then I heard whistling as if a missile had blown low over my head. There was a thump as a winged figure hove into view and lifted the hierophant from his saddle, bearing him away into the strange welkin wherein loomed the argent lunar orb that had lured us here.

"Nay!" I shouted, but before I could stop him, Abnon the archer had already sent a volley speeding into the night sky. The arrow found its mark, and the winged one faltered, plummeting earthward and dropping its prey. Hierophant and arcane staff separated and hurtled toward us far below. I watched with gritted teeth as the hierophant fell to his inexorable doom. He flailed his arms and almost seemed to shift shape as his voluminous robes fluttered in the light of the great metallic moon, but there was no time to witness his death, for another of the things lighted on Abnon and drove him onto his back.

Asenthine and I wrenched swords from scabbards, and even as we did, we heard the sickening wet sound of the winged one wrenching the heart from Abnon's chest. The head of the demoniacal creature turned a curious glance upon Asenthine, the abbot, and me. Large red eyes like rubies were set back in an alabaster feminine face framed by long straight sable locks. She regarded the three of us curiously as she devoured the archer's heart with relish. Fangs like the teeth of a great jungle cat shewed pearly in the beams of that wicked eldritch moon.

With a smile she mocked us as her ribbed leathern wings twitched and fluttered. Abnon was dead, but I had it in my mind to avenge him. Asenthine seemed to reckon the same, but before we could move forward, another of the winged devil-women alighted on Asenthine's back with a loud thump and dug her claws into him. The succubus screamed her awful cry and started to take to the skies with the vampyre, but before she had lifted him far from his saddle, he grabbed her by her long black tresses and flung her over his head. The abomination hit the ground and came back up, giant bat-like wings beating the air in anger.

I carried the attack to the feasting demoness who sat on the dead body of the archer, eating his heart. I slashed at the succubus, a feint, then with a two-handed thrust I drove my broadsword into a veiny wing. I wrenched my glaive free and felt the wind from her razor-sharp talon as she barely missed digging into my throat. I hacked into her other wing. She let out a cry and leapt on me, knocking me to the ground. Her raptor-like talons again sought my throat, but I managed to bring my arms over her upper arms and under. I took a deep breath and flung my arms wide. She was fast, and I was going to have to finish this quickly, else I was a dead man. Like a flash of levin, my hand shot to the dagger at my baldric and drove upwards into her sternum, me betting everything that her heart—if she had one—occupied the same space as mine. I felt the succubus go limp and I got my boot between us and kicked her from me. And still she attacked, albeit much slower, slow enough that before she could throw up any sort of defense, I had hacked into her neck with one blow and sent her head spinning from her body like a top. The demoness' body folded its crippled wings, then toppled to the ground.

I turned to see Asenthine still engaged in battle with his assailant. From behind the demoness, the abbot pelted her with rocks and what looked like rotten fruit, though where he found it, I have no idea. Asenthine still fought the succubus from horseback, his rapier locked in a deadly dance with the fangs and talons of the creature while he turned his mount this way and that. Both vampyre and succubus bled from myriad wounds, but both seemed to possess their full strength. The horned winged creature fluttered her sable vans and dipped in again. With a decisive thrust, Asenthine drove the point of his rapier into her heart. The succubus alighted on her talons, and I raced in behind her and slashed. Her head fell from her shoulders as she beat her wings and began to take to the air, then collapsed to the ground.

Asenthine and I were breathing laboriously from our exertions. I nodded and said as I gasped for breath, "The head. It's always the head to stop things like that. It's why I prefer this." I twitched my fingers over the blade of my ensanguined broadsword.

Asenthine thrust his bloody rapier into his scabbard and said, "Well, put that meat cleaver up. We need—" But he was interrupted by hooves that clattered on the cobblestone streets of Darkling

Reich.

Though we stole only glances out of the corners of our eyes for fear of the intoxicating and debilitating effects of looking upon that strange angular architecture that lined the streets of Darkling Reich, we recognized that we seemed to be in the heart of the sinister city now. Herein, avenues crisscrossed and lay labyrinthine in all directions. Again, the sinister hoofbeats beat the cobblestone streets back and forth, but we saw no one illumined by the great metallic moon that glistened wetly like mercury. The moon had ceased receding, and I surmised we had arrived at the destination wherein it had intended to lead us, like a carrot dangled before the snout of a hungry beast.

Anon, a blade slashed my arm and with the return caught Asenthine across his back. We hadn't heard the knight's approach but saw his mount recede down the avenue across from us, his mount's hoofbeats kicking up a delayed echo. I felt myself growing weary, weary unto death. I remembered a dream, a recurring dream in which Death stalked me and I had died. A dream in which I became weaker and weaker until I fell into eternal oblivion. One of the few times in my life I had known genuine fear was just now. I sank into eternal impotence and slid involuntarily from my mount. I woke with a thud upon the ground, sank again into total darkness, and woke once again to find Wrathmane, the abbot, Asenthine, and their mounts gone.

I found my feet and drew my broadsword, weaving and staggering. I didn't hear the hoofbeats until the knight had ridden by and slashed me across my face. Only lightning reflexes prevented it from being a fatal blow, but I was well aware that the knight in his armor of polished jet was toying with me. I could hear his laughter, amplified tenfold as he rode off down the alleyway.

I stumbled along, weary unto death and diminished to impotence by Death incarnate that was the Knight of Darkling Reich. I was alone in a world within a world that was not the world I knew.

Was I to die this far from home? And alone? Forgotten? Killed by Death on a quest to save the world, a quest that had amounted to nothing. Every sound was amplified. Every sound echoed. My weakened heart raced, and my body shook. At one point the trembling started to subside, whereupon for a length of time the knight seemed to have gone away. It was as if he had never existed—that is, until I felt his sword slash my thigh, and I crumbled to the ground.

Rising, I stumbled through this maze of torment that was the streets of Darkling Reich, mocked by an assassin who could have killed me any moment he chose yet rather seemed to derive perverse pleasure from my prolonged suffering. My armor was rent and my garments were in tatters. I had lost much blood. Only when I dropped upon the ground to sink into eternal slumber like a man trapped in a boreal world who gasps his last few gelid breaths before lying on the tundra to expire had I realized I had dropped my sword. It lay yards away. The knight was standing over me. His cachinnations reverberated as he raised his sword for the killing blow. Unable to move and with eyelids half-opened, I saw a stealthy phosphorescent arc that illuminated a great bird of prey alighting behind him. I was as one in the throes of sleep paralysis, and I waited on the quietus, but it never came. The green effulgence lashed out and struck the knight's casque. I heard a sizzle. The knight headed over onto the ground like a mannequin, as if the assassin who had been Death itself had never existed as an animate thing.

Through my dim and hazy gaze, I saw Hegumen Hordane the Hierophant and the Abbot Eothoclemes. A clatter of horse's hooves, and Asenthine rode up on his steed holding Wrathmane by the reins beside of him. From behind the hierophant and the abbot a figure riding pillion with Asenthine dismounted and sauntered forward. The thing was a pitiful emaciated creature, stringy red locks obscuring its face. Slowly raising her bowed head, she struggled to remain erect. Recognition seemed to slowly return to her haunted emerald eyes. "K-Karnov…" she stammered.

"D'vartha!" I gasped and sank into black oblivion.

Chapter VII
That Night in Darkling Reich

After many days of fever dreams in which I was stalked by a great black shape that was Death itself, I now sat around the circular table in the feasting hall of the abbey with my companions. We quaffed foaming jacks of ale as they recounted that night in Darkling Reich.

The hierophant spoke. "Had it not been for you keeping the Knight of Darkling Reich at bay whilst I found D'vartha and performed the exorcism, I fear we would not be sitting here discussing it now."

"I saw you fall from the sky when Abnon's arrow plunged into the succubus that had borne you aloft, though I did not see you strike the ground. I presumed you dead," I said

He chuckled. "A man may die when he falls from the sky, but not an eagle. I transformed into the mighty raptor ere I could hit the ground. I retrieved my staff and flew with it in my beak until I sighted the gravemound on the hillside in which D'vartha slept, immured as she was, deep within, while the knight did the demoniacal bidding of Yr."

D'vartha spoke. "Once the husk of Yr had entered me, she became only stronger and stronger. I was deceived by the head of Xycanthia to traverse the depths of the tilted runes and suffered the bouleversement that ensued. You said the oracle now sleeps under the hierophant's spell. Remind me to burn her accursed head before we leave. The corrupted Yr used me as a vessel to carry out her malevolent agenda—to traverse Time and plunge creation into chaos by the subversion of the male manifestation of order and pave the way for the feminine in chaos, bringing back the All-Night."

The hierophant nodded. "Though our world is neither the beginning nor the ending of Time—as there really is none—by the husk of Yr's calculations, our here and now is the starting point to set the end, as we perceive it, in motion."

"I thought I was dealing with the Yr rune, but it was the husk of the rune—corrupted and perverse—that possessed me," D'vartha said to us. "Had Hordane not rescued me from being buried alive and performed the exorcism, I would have starved to death and rotted in my casket. For surely the knight saw me as a plaything only and was already losing interest in me."

"What was he?" I asked. "For I've surely never encountered such a formidable foe before, a man who cannot even be struck, let alone vanquished, by weapons of steel."

"He was not a man," D'vartha said. "He was an opposing force of creation itself, a runic manifestation of Death mocking man in human form, although he was given an ego and masculine desires when he was shaped on the physical plane. When Hordane struck the knight with his staff and banished the runic force, his armor fell onto the ground in pieces, with no sign of a man who had worn it. Then the armor melted into tarry piles and disintegrated."

"As I scanned the expanse of Darkling Reich on the wings of the eagle, I saw no sight of you at first, Karnov, only Asenthine and Eothoclemes, wandering the labyrinthine maze in which you had vanished," the hierophant said.

Asenthine nodded. "It was as if you vanished into the ether, Karnov. The knight had veiled you in the blackness of death, where we could not find you. The hierophant found me and called me away. With the help of the servitors he called forth with his arcane staff, we dug up D'vartha, and he exorcised her. You would not believe the device the knight had designed to send air down to D'vartha's buried body. It even defies the scientific knowledge of my own people."

D'vartha shuddered.

The hierophant spoke. "Once I had exhumed D'vartha's body, I bound the Yr rune and searched Darkling Reich through the eyes of the knight. It wasn't long before I found your location in the maze, and in good time. I quickly performed the exorcism and guided our companions on the wings of the eagle you saw alight just before I hurled the Knight of Darkling Reich back into the darkness that begat him by the gramarye of my staff."

"I fear creation itself remains in grave danger, D'vartha," said Asenthine. "We must make haste and return to our world and point in time, and regain the power of the Cosmic Ice. You must use your mastery of the Demonic Trinity to reinstate Karnov's powers of the Cosmic Ice, for not only is the world now threatened with vampyric sovereignty, but the Queen of the Earthly Demonic, Esmadrunga, is now enthralled by the sorcerer, Nesodomntha. The very balance of chaos and order is yet again in a most perilous position."

D'vartha's emerald eyes widened, then drew tight again like those of a cat. I could tell she was ruminating over all that we had said. It was a great deal for me to think about, as well.

"Will you come with us, Hegumen Hordane the Hierophant?" I asked. "We could use your wisdom and mastery of the arcane staff."

"No. I must stay here. As your wyrd is to be the Rider of the Cosmic Ice in your world, so is mine to be the guardian of this realm. But as it is the way of chaos and order, and gods and demons to ever dice with the fate of men, our paths may very well cross again."

I nodded my understanding and drained my drinking jack. Then I called for another. I was ready to plunge back into the mêlée against whatever forces threatened mankind. Just give me time to quaff but one more ale, and the wicked would fall before my blade!

Book III
By Byron A. Roberts

Chapter I
A Reclamation of Power and a Recollection of Sorrow

I stood alone at the edge of the labyrinthine forest, gazing into the shadowed depths of the sylvan verdure and brooding upon the events of the past several days. Not two hours ago, the crimson-tressed witch D'vartha had completed the arcane rite of transformation and once more imbued me with the eldritch might of the Cosmic Ice, empowering my battle-scarred frame with the ancient sorcery which would again enable me to assimilate the perfidious souls of the undead. As I glanced at the faint tendrils of cerulean energy which danced and shimmered wanly upon the surface of my rune-etched armour, I found myself pondering the secrets of the hoary might which I so potently wielded. Although I still knew scant little of the enchantment's nature beyond the cryptic fragments D'vartha had divulged concerning its origin being irrevocably linked to the mysterious soul-magicks of the Demonic Trinity, I nevertheless felt exultant to once more experience the primal energy which its embrace afforded me. At the same time, I was grimly aware that the ceaseless thirst of my ensorcelled mantle would undoubtedly demand to be slaked before long. Indeed, it seemed like an eternity since my adamantine blade had cloven vampyric flesh and channelled the malefic spirits of the night-spawn into my ice-clad thews. Silently, at the periphery of that benighted woodland, I solemnly vowed that the nefarious Nesadomntha and his aberrant horde of Niaughu fiends would soon suffer the ire of the Phantom-Clad Rider, and pitiless indeed would be the dire and dreadful wrath of Karnov!

With a weary sigh I fixed my gaze upon the gibbous moon

which glowered down upon the arboreal vault like a baleful, silvern eye. Our journey back across the interdimensional threshold had been inestimably less perilous than our accursed trek to the blighted Plain of Gnathongules, for our path home had been clearly mapped for us with the indispensable aid of Hegumen Hordane the Hierophant and his powerful magicks. So precise had been the sage's eldritch cartography that he had been able to conjure a mystic gateway directly to the southern expanse of Duros Zuil where the trackless woodlands met the trade routes leading to the cities of the coastal fiefdoms. Reflecting now upon the morning of our sojourn, I reached into the leather pouch at my belt and brought forth a small, multifaceted crystal which glimmered with a wan, sapphirean luminescence. The gem had been given to me by the Hierophant immediately prior to our departure, and as I peered into the stone's lambent depths, I recalled the words he had spoken to me mere moments before we plunged headlong into the fulgid portal between worlds...

"Karnov, take this gem. It will aid you in your impending and direful struggle against the forces of darkness. This stone has been infused with powerful sorcery, imbuing it with the ability to cast out any malign spirit which has deigned to take possession of an innocent host, duly cleansing that soul of corruption and banishing any invasive eidolon to the black reaches of the chaosphere. My ensorcelled stave is studded with gems such as this, and ever do they serve me well in my rites of exorcism, for the energumen fiends of the abyssal void are invariably reluctant to vacate their mortal vessels. Now, go! You must not tarry. The turmoil wrought upon this realm by your red witch D'vartha was considerable, and there are many here who would see her swinging from the gallows for the madness she unleashed upon the land, unwittingly or not! Farewell!"

Grim of visage, I duly returned the stone to my belt pouch and strode sullenly to the makeshift camp which I and my traveling companions had established at the frontier of the dense forest. The vampyric nobleman Asenthine sat silently before our blazing fire, his eyes closed and his head bowed as if in deep meditation. The lithe warrior's slender rapier was at his side and his thin lips bore an ensanguined hue, for he had recently fed upon the blood of some hapless woodland beast. Even bathed by the rutilant glow of the dancing flames, I mused that the man's gaunt face unerringly retained its deathly pale pallor. My hulking steed Wrathmane was tethered nearby to a gnarled yew tree, silent and content from his reacquisition of the same spectral power as that which sustained me. The benevolent Abbot Eothoclemes had furnished us with meagre provisions for both human and equine consumption before our departure from his realm, and we had gratefully availed ourselves of those victuals as the dusk had yielded grudgingly to the night upon our return.

The sound of stealthy footsteps suddenly drew my attention and I turned to see the witch D'vartha slinking toward me from the tenebrous shadows of the foliage. She was clad in a figure-hugging, green woollen dress and doeskin boots, the garments having been graciously bestowed upon her by the Abbot and his attendants as a replacement for the tattered and mouldering rags which she had sported during her period of possession-induced madness. The lissom woman's tousled tresses seemed to shine an even deeper shade of crimson in the undulating light of the campfire and her beguiling eyes sparkled like twin emeralds.

"I must rest now," the witch purred. "The rite of the Cosmic Ice was taxing for me, and I must replenish my energies. The lost facet of your power has been returned to you, but be aware that the enchantment differs subtly from that which you formerly wielded due to certain fluctuations in the patterns of the chthonic web."

"What do you mean?" I asked guardedly.

"The mana of the Threefold Covenant is a living entity, Karnov. Each incarnation of it is unique. The way in which it manifests may be malleable, ebbing and flowing like an eldritch tide."

I scowled. "I am none the wiser, D'vartha."

The witch rolled her eyes. "Suffice it to say that the effects of absorbing and shaping the soul-force of the undead may shift with whichever aspect of the demonic balance is currently in the ascendancy. That is all I can tell you. Now, do try not to lose your power again, Karnov Ice-Blade."

I nodded at the beauteous woman. "Be assured, enchantress… I shall strive not to divest myself of it in the future."

A sly smile curled the witch's fulsome lips. "Just as I shall strive not to relinquish my hold on the reins of sanity henceforth."

"Indeed," I growled. "Across two worlds, you left a trail of lunacy and chaos in your wake. You were lucky to escape that realm with your life. I cannot fathom what manner of delirium took hold of your mind while you were possessed by that accursed succubus."

The woman's delicate brow furrowed in mock indignation. "Oh dear, are you chastising me, Karnov? Surely I cannot be held solely responsible for the rune-spirit's malign plot to traverse the filaments of time and orchestrate the corruption of man's vaunted divinity?"

My icy eyes narrowed as I regarded the winsome witch. "Did the spirit sow that debased seed in you, I wonder? Or did it merely cultivate and nurture a notion which already existed within your devious mind?"

The witch laughed, the sound melodious and colder than hoarfrost. "My dear Karnov, you shall doubtless never know! But it's a universal axiom that the female of the species is far more deadly than the male." With that, D'vartha moved to a rough-spun woollen blanket which was laid out next to the fire and slowly reclined upon it. Beside her was the ornate wooden box which still contained the gangrenous, severed head of the vampyress Xycanthia.

"Why the hell did you bring that thrice-cursed thing back with you?" I grumbled as I moved to the fire and seated myself before its warming glow. "I thought you said you were going to burn it!"

D'vartha smiled mirthlessly. "Oh, I have something far more effective in mind to dispose of my beloved sister's earthly remains. That duplicitous bitch deceived me and set me upon a harrowing path of madness and depravity. I mean to repay her tenfold for her base treachery!"

"Well, keep the reeking thing quiet. I don't want to hear that head start prattling again."

"Fear not, Karnov. The hierophant's spell of slumber yet endures. It will be some time before she awakens."

I sighed deeply. "And you will keep your vow to journey with us to the lair of Nesadomntha and the foetid mound of Esmadrunga? Your sorcerous skills would be a great asset in the coming battle."

"I have duly sworn that oath," the witch hissed. "Judging by what you have told me, that deluded necromancer has dared enthrall an avatar of the Earthly Demonic and bend her divine power to his black will. For deigning to defile the sanctity of the chthonic pantheon I am honour-bound to see him pay dearly for his affront to the ancient ways."

"Good! The last time that bloated thing had me in its clutches, it drained me of my sigaldry. And my steel couldn't even pierce its feculent hide! I have scant little desire to lay eyes on that heaving, repugnant mass again, I can tell you!"

D'vartha sighed in exasperation. "Well, of course you couldn't harm her, you lumbering oaf. You're a man! And one whose power is at least partially derived from the same source, to boot!"

"Is that so?" I muttered.

"Naturally, Karnov," the witch continued. "When dealing with the feminine aspect of the Earthly Demonic, the bumbling, heavy-handed approach of your gender will avail us naught. Such things require the finesse of a woman's touch. Rest assured, this falls solely within my purview. Leave Esmadrunga to me."

I watched D'vartha as she closed her viridian eyes and fell into a fitful slumber. The fabric of her dress shifted subtly to reveal the eburnean flesh of her thighs and it was some time before I was able to tear my gaze from that alluring sight. When I finally glanced back at the fire, I suddenly descried that Asenthine had emerged from his meditative state and was now staring intently at me from across the writhing flames.

"That witch has a sharp tongue," he growled.

"And a sharp mind to match it," I replied. "Her arcane might is not to be underestimated. We will require her skills when next we face Nesadomntha."

"I don't doubt it," muttered Asenthine. "This will be our last throw of the die, Karnov. That scurrilous devil will not have been idle during our sojourn beyond the dimensional veil. He will most assuredly have spawned a myriad more of his accursed hybrid abominations. And I'll warrant he will have bolstered his defences against any who would dare aspire to thwart his nefarious schemes."

"I pray you are right, Asenthine," I hissed. "I long for the embrace of battle once more. Know that I shall blacken my blade in the thick of the fray and rejoice in every impure soul that my enchantment devours!"

Asenthine nodded silently and stared into the undulating flames, apparently lost in thought. Then, he suddenly levelled his gaze at me and spoke. "We both experienced harrowing visions within the Tunnel of Sorrows. Just what did that vile place show you, Karnov?"

"You would pry into a man's deepest regrets and most dolorous woes?" I gnarred. "Nay. I shall keep my own silent counsel regarding that blighted labyrinth of despair!"

"As you wish."

"Mayhap you desire to share your own visions of grief?" I asked guardedly. "I heard you cry out at the loss of your family whilst in that withering purgatory."

Asenthine's pallid brow furrowed. "Aye, that charnel-pit compelled me to relive the cruellest losses and betrayals of my life. And when you have lived as long as I have, the bitter wellspring of woe from which that place drew was deep indeed."

"Countless centuries of sorrow," I muttered. "A truly tortuous ordeal, I'll wager."

"To be sure," the vampyre said solemnly. "And yet, one of the most pitiless visions was also one of the most recent. The freshest wounds are the most painful, I suppose. You recall what I told you of the vampyre concubine, Noctivia? The one who aided me in my escape from Ghormanteia's lair?"

"I do."

"As you know, I manipulated that beauteous creature without mercy, wielding my Alunai powers of persuasion and seduction to wholly bend her to my will. The poor wench was so smitten with me that she would have willingly faced the Final Death to ensure my liberation."

"A deft and prudent use of your powers," I ventured.

"Indeed," whispered Asenthine. "But there was an unexpected consequence born of the covenant which I induced between Noctivia and myself. So intense was our liaison that I found myself developing feelings for her in response. I loved her, Karnov!"

"Love, was it?" I grumbled. "Not infatuation, or simply lust?"

"Nay! Despite the circumstances of my incarceration, I knew that I was in love with that hapless girl, and yet nevertheless I continued to manipulate her without mercy, for I was concerned only with my ultimate goal… that being to facilitate my freedom at all costs."

"You acted out of necessity, Asenthine," I said. "In truth, I know scant little of the nature of trysts which may exist between the undead, but you should not berate yourself so. You had no choice."

Asenthine sighed heavily. "In the end, I abandoned her to Ghormanteia's pitiless vengeance. I knew that he would undoubtedly discover Noctivia's betrayal and visit upon her a retribution so terrible that I could not begin to fathom the magnitude of its cruelty. But still I fled from that atramentous fortress without a backward glance, heedless of the girl's desperate pleas that I take her with me. I simply left her to die."

Scowling, I took up a goatskin gourd from beside the campfire and swallowed a draught of Abbot Eothoclemes' spiced wine. Then, I fixed the morose Asenthine with a steely glare. "She was but a vampyre, and her death was no great loss. And be aware that I mean no offence to thee by that remark. But you know the veracity of my words as well as I do. Now, rouse yourself from this damnable morass of self-pity and prepare for the coming battle!"

For many moments, Asenthine stared at me, his eyes sparkling in the light from the flames. Finally, he spoke, his voice scarcely more than a whisper. "I wonder, Karnov... who in truth is the more bereft of humanity... you or the inhuman fiends you have vowed so solemnly to destroy?"

I smiled coldly. "An incisive question, Asenthine. Perhaps we shall discover the answer together, once our foes lie rent and riven at our feet."

Chapter II
Of Dreams and Declarations of Vengeance

I stood alone upon a blighted, niveous plateau, entwined by the ephemeral tendrils of a vivid and portentous dream. Above me, a baleful moon glowered from the benighted sky, its lambent light imbuing the frosty vista with a ghostly radiance. Gazing into the depths of the snow-shrouded dreamscape, I suddenly beheld a lone figure emerge from the boreal mists and take up a silent vigil upon the hiemal plain. The towering eidolon stood deathly still, akin to a great sentinel carved from the very heart of the primeval ice. As I stared at the dolent figure, I descried with some surprise that it was evidently clad in the same spectral armour as that which encased my own mortal frame, its face similarly concealed by a rimy and chalybeous helm. With astonishing speed, the silent paladin hefted a mighty ice-encrusted battle-axe and proceeded to drive the scintillant weapon deep into the frozen earth. Abruptly, a blossom of azure light leaped from the glyph-scored steel and a sound not unlike distant thunder reverberated throughout the ice-bound vista. Instantly, as if in answer to the thunder's clarion, there appeared from the mist two ranks of armoured knights, their steel-clad heads bowed in reverence, their fulgent swords held solemnly before them as if in wordless prayer. The serried templars stood silently at my flanks as if enacting the rite of some grim and time-lost pageant, all of them as still and sombre as carven effigies. Slowly, I levelled my gaze at the brooding figure which stood at the head of the eldritch procession and watched as it raised a gauntleted hand. Then, the paladin spoke, its voice as resonant as a peal of thunder and yet as soft as a sibilant whisper…

"Karnov! Stand you ready to learn the secrets of the Cosmic Ice and the true nature of the power which you wield?"

My throat was tight with anticipation, and yet I found my reply. "I am ready!"

The stentorian voice boomed again, louder than before. "Know now that the ancient lore of the Brotherhood of the Ensanguined Ice may ravage you and lash your mind like a vessel upon a storm-wracked sea! Will you yet receive the forbidden knowledge of the Threefold Covenant?"

"I will!"

"So be it!" the paladin thundered. "Then wait, and watch. Continue your grim crusade against the vile legions of those who walk in death. When the blood moon rises to herald the ascent of the Demonic Trinity, then shall the secrets of the phantom templars be divulged to you. Now, Karnov... awaken!"

I awoke with a jolt to find myself beneath a towering oak as the first light of dawn painted the sky with rutilant hues. Some yards distant, my party's campfire guttered, its flames slowly dying with the retreat of the night. There was no sign of D'vartha or Asenthine, but my steed Wrathmane stood silently in the shadows of the yew tree's boughs where I had tethered him. I rose wearily and made ready to venture forth from our sylvan sanctuary, adjusting my chainmail hauberk and buckling on my cuirass. Methodically, I strapped my vambraces to my forearms and secured my mount's saddlebags before commencing to hone my ancestral broadsword's blade with a whetstone. A stealthy footfall from the tree line at my back suddenly compelled me to turn and I beheld D'vartha emerge briskly from the depths of the forest. The witch had evidently fashioned for herself a staff, hewn from the bough of an ash tree and engraved with elaborate runes and arcane sigils. Her snow-pale face was adorned with streaks of woad and her viridian eyes sparkled with a steely resolve. At her hip rested a leather sheath containing a slender dagger with a hilt of polished ivory, presumably purloined from amongst Asenthine's sizeable collection of weapons. I realized in an instant that the fey enchantress had donned the mantle of battle, embracing that most martial and fearsome facet of her protean nature, that of the War-Witch.

"You are suitably girt for the fray," I grumbled, scabbarding my sword.

D'vartha smiled coyly. "In more ways than you know, Karnov."

"Heed me, woman. Last night I dreamt of the Cosmic Ice, and those who have borne its power before me. I have glimpsed them but once before... during my very first sojourn through the frozen labyrinth of that spectral domain. I was told that the secrets of this ageless sorcery would be revealed to me in due course."

"Indeed?" the witch replied, her brow arching quizzically.

"Is there anything you would care to divulge to me concerning this vision?"

"The Cosmic Ice is a nexus for many things, Karnov. Light and darkness, salvation and damnation. The beginning and the end of all journeys awaits a traveller within that eldritch hinterland. Beware you do not delve too deeply in your quest for revelation, for you may not like everything you find along that parlous path."

"Bloody riddles and cryptic nonsense!" I growled, vaulting to Wrathmane's broad back. "I should have known not to expect a straight answer from a witch!"

D'vartha grinned, brushing a lock of crimson hair from before her eyes. "Well, we Daughters of the Welkin Coven can't reveal all our deepest secrets to mere mortals, can we?"

"Where is Asenthine?" I asked with a scowl.

"Scouting the road east," replied D'vartha, taking up the ornate box which contained her sister's head and placing it into a hessian sack which she then slung carelessly across her shoulder. "He said he would rendezvous with us before the sun reaches its zenith."

"Come then," I muttered, grasping the woman's slender arm and hauling her roughly into the saddle behind me. "Let us ride forth and see what sublime horrors Nesadomntha has prepared for us. And with any luck, I'll sup deep of a few more unclean souls before the sun sets!"

* * *

For many hours we rode east, glimpsing not another living soul upon the desolate road. With each onerous mile we traversed, the verdant forest flanking the trail yielded ever more grudgingly before the encroaching marshland of Karagh-Ghul. At length, as the veiled sun rose to its apex, the wide roadway dwindled to nothing more than a bemired track until finally it gave way completely to a broad expanse of noisome swamp. With a scowl I reined Wrathmane to a halt.

"The stench of black sigaldry carries far," whispered D'vartha, shifting irritably in the saddle behind me. "But it seems we are not alone at the frontier of this blighted place."

At the perimeter of the quagmire ahead I suddenly spied the red-cloaked figure of Asenthine, standing as silent and immobile as a graven statue. The lithe swordsman gazed impassively out across the vast morass, one hand resting upon the hilt of his slender rapier. After several moments, he turned slowly to face us.

"Nesadomntha has not been idle," the Alunai nobleman grumbled. "The ranks of the Niaughu have been bolstered by a legion of newly spawned abominations."

"This news does not surprise me," I replied sullenly. "What else has your scouting expedition revealed?"

"My inhuman eyes see far. I ventured some way into the swamp, and grim were the events which I beheld."

"Enlighten us, Asenthine."

"A retinue of knights from the Grand Duchy south of Zukatia rode to investigate reports of the nefarious activity within this region. They encountered and slew a contingent of the necromancer's cultists at the frontier of the marsh. But then they made the grave error of venturing deeper into the mire. This morning, the knights were massacred by the Niaughu. None survived."

"Fie!" I exclaimed. "Damn those accursed devils!"

"The Niaughu are indeed a diabolical aberration," mused D'vartha as she climbed swiftly down from Wrathmane's back. "The dubious gift of their birthright from Esmadrunga affords them certain arcane advantages."

"Aye, a most peculiar breed of vampyre," I said, levelling my gaze slowly at Asenthine. "But then, so are your own Alunai forebears, judging by what you have told me."

"I hope for your sake you are not likening my vaunted brethren to those Niaughu vermin," growled Asenthine.

"Not at all," I replied evenly. "I merely find the diversity of your kind surprising."

"There are numerous races amongst the Ordo Vampyrica," muttered Asenthine coldly. "The abilities and dispositions of the elder blood-clans vary greatly. But the Niaughu are an impure and debased creation. They are wholly unnatural."

"Some would argue that the very notion of benevolent vampyres such as the Alunai is itself an unnatural postulation," I said with a wry smile.

D'vartha abruptly cast a cautionary glare at me, which I duly ignored.

Asenthine merely sighed wistfully. "The secrets of the Alunai are myriad, Karnov. Once, long ago, we presided over our ethereal realm in serene and benevolent glory. The cloud-capped minarets of Seika Heime shone like purest gold kissed by the sun and our aegis was supreme and unopposed."

I nodded ruminatively. "Perhaps all kingdoms inevitably fall prey to their own hubris."

Anger suddenly flared in Asenthine's eyes. "Hubris? You dare speak ill of the Alunai's legacy? We were akin to gods! Divine avatars amongst the Great Houses of the noble vampyre bloodlines!"

"Undoubtedly," I ventured. "But gods deprived of worship inevitably become nothing more than myths. At any rate, we cannot tarry here bickering about lost divinity. We have more pressing concerns… such as deciding how best to overcome our foe."

"I shall weave a spell of concealment about us," said D'vartha. "Our approach to Nesadomntha's reeking sanctum shall be cloaked by magicks, if naught else."

"'Tis a pity that we can gather no allies in this endeavour," gnarred Asenthine. "But in truth this is devilish work, not suited to the frailty of humans."

"Then it falls to us to end this unholy scourge," I enounced. "We shall ride forth into that vile mere and purify it with steel and sorcery!"

"Bold words, Karnov," whispered D'vartha. "And while it is true that no mortal warband exists to aid us, not all armies are raised from the realms of men."

"What does that mean?" I queried guardedly.

D'vartha smiled. "Suffice it to say that you shall yet witness the heavy toll which is exacted when the Earthly Demonic is manipulated by such a corrupt and sinister hand as Nesadomntha's."

"More riddles!" I hissed. "You've a serpent's tongue behind those ruby lips, I swear it!"

Asenthine scowled suddenly with vexation. "If only my steed Merklethenon were here. It would make this damnable trek less of an ordeal."

"That truculent beast is most likely devouring livestock at a distant farm somewhere," I said mordantly. "But perhaps you could transform a passing goat into your next mount?"

The Alunai nobleman remained dour of countenance as he fixed me with a withering glare. "Your wit is truly peerless, human."

"Enough prattle!" I said, glancing skywards. The midday sun was all but obscured by a cinereous vault of brooding cloud. "It will be dusk by the time we reach the demon's barrow. But I vow that blasted necromancer's demented plot to unleash the hordes of the Niaughu upon mankind shall be thwarted!"

"Know this, Karnov," growled Asenthine, his pallid brow furrowing. "Nesadomntha is mine. I will wreak my vengeance upon that revenant for the role he played in the decimation of my people, and the blow which ends his foul life shall be dealt by me alone."

A mirthless grin crept across my face as I studied the vampyric warrior. "Of course, Asenthine. Far be it from me to stand in the way of a man and his revenge."

Chapter III
And the Earth Shall Disgorge Its Wrathful Legions! (The Battle of the Marsh: Part I)

Our journey into the dank embrace of Karagh-Ghul's miry interior was vile, yet uneventful. D'vartha's enchantment ensured that we were hidden from the eyes of Nesadomntha's thralls and also served to keep at bay the more ferine and ravenous denizens of the feculent swamp. Wrathmane's tireless advance through the marsh was slow but unerring, and Asenthine's vampyric constitution served him well as he leapt nimbly from the gnarled and blackened boughs of the innumerable vine-shackled trees which thronged the humid morass. The incessant chittering and keening of the slough's malign fauna rose in intensity with each onerous yard we traversed until it was akin to a maddening and ceaseless cacophony in our ears. At length, as the moon languorously supplanted the sun in the darkling sky, we at last found ourselves overlooking the vast swale wherein the barrow of Esmadrunga sat brooding like the rotting carcass of some moss-encrusted titan of primeval myth. A score of Niaughu swarmed dementedly over the surface of the mound like colossal ants, while several of the batrachian creatures which served as Nesadomntha's minions squatted silently within the foetid bog, their bulbous eyes wide and unblinking. D'vartha and I swiftly dismounted and crept closer to survey the hive. Silent as a ghost, Asenthine then leaped from the twisted bough of a towering tree and moved stealthily to my side. His crimson cloak was befouled by the muck of the mire and his eyes seemed to glow with a simmering rage.

"We must draw Nesadomntha out from that foul subterrane," hissed the Alunai swordsman.

I nodded grimly. "The clamour of battle shall serve in that regard, I'll wager."

D'vartha hefted her ensorcelled staff and studied the black barrow. "While you engage those creatures, I shall seek a path into the mound and strive to liberate Esmadrunga from the necromancer's spell."

"And what if you require our aid within that verminous vault of ghouls?" I asked. "How will we know how you fare in those benighted depths?"

D'vartha sighed exasperatedly and reached out to lift the lucent visor of my helm. Then she placed her fingers lightly upon my forehead and closed her eyes. At once, I felt a strange sensation of tingling cold envelop my brow.

"There," the witch said, swiftly withdrawing her hand. "For a time, there shall be a sorcerous link between us. You have but to picture me in your mind's eye, and for a fleeting moment you shall possess the ability to see through my eyes. Although I very much doubt that I shall require your assistance, Karnov."

"So be it, woman," I assented grudgingly.

The crimson-tressed sorceress then proceeded to remove the severed head of Xycanthia from its box and tie the grisly object unceremoniously to her belt by the strands of its own slimy, matted hair. Bloated maggots dropped from the greying flesh and the pale eyes set within the decaying skull seemed to gaze out unnervingly as if in mute malice.

I scowled in disgust. "Again I ask, why must you cart that hideous thing about? What exactly are you going to do with it?"

D'vartha smiled coldly. "If you must know, I'm going to feed it to Esmadrunga. Consider it something of a sanctified burial, if you will. And after my sister's debasement of the Earthly Demonic energies, such an act will also have an element of poetic justice about it, don't you think?"

"Whatever you say," I grumbled.

"My spell of concealment shall be lifted in mere moments," the witch rasped. "But I shall perform another rite forthwith... an invocation which will even the odds in this battle significantly!"

And with that, D'vartha disappeared into the writhing shadows of the mire.

"She's touched by moon-madness, I'll warrant," grumbled Asenthine disdainfully.

"Mayhap," I replied. "But I'm thankful she's here with us, regardless."

Asenthine shook his head and proceeded to creep closer to the edge of the marsh. With his black cuirass glinting in the moonlight, he seemed to traverse the foliage with the preternatural stealth of a wraith.

Doffing my cloak, I turned to my silent steed Wrathmane and patted his glistening flank. "Stay back, my friend. Engage such fiends as seek to waylay you, but do not venture any closer to the mound. Your great size will not serve you well in that treacherous mire."

I made to unfasten my war-scored shield from the barding's steel-plated crupper, but swiftly thought better of it; the impending battle would require the two-handed arc of my broadsword and I therefore decided to sacrifice defence in favour of a harrowing and pitiless whirlwind of steel.

Suddenly, the voice of D'vartha crested the clamour of the teeming swamp. Her words of invocation were uttered in a tongue beyond my ken, but I knew instantly that the spell she intoned was born of the ancient chthonic grimoires of the Earthly Demonic. Turning swiftly to gaze at the barrow, I descried the Niaughu fiends abruptly cease their movement and lift their squamous faces to the sky, evidently enthralled by the sound of the sibilant rite. Scant seconds later, the marsh before the great mound began to undulate and churn, as if it were an ocean disturbed by a tempestuous gale. The surface of the mire then commenced to bubble and roil, emitting thick plumes of viridian vapour. My eyes widened in astonishment as I duly beheld the first of D'vartha's conjured vassals rise languorously from the foetid bog. A creature cast crudely in the semblance of a man, its body was evidently composed of the very mire itself. The paludal golem sported a skin of viscous moss and lichen, its sinews seemingly crafted of knurled roots and twisted vines. Its muculent muscles rippled fluidly and a plethora of worms and insects writhed within the verdurous latticework of its hulking frame. Sporting a tuberous face devoid of features and twin black hollows wherein no eyes dwelt, the muck-encrusted mockery of a man finally hauled its steaming bulk triumphantly from the marsh. And all around the fibrous effigy, more of its misshapen ilk were rising from the quagmire and slowly assuming formation before the brooding barrow of Esmadrunga. I could scarcely fathom the magnitude of the sorcerous power which animated those grotesquely shambling creatures, but when I glanced to the eastern edge of the swale, I acknowledged in a heartbeat the undeniable might of the woman who had marshalled them. D'vartha emerged from the shadows like a demigoddess of myth, her magicks bearing her aloft so that she glided effortlessly above the surface of the marsh. Her crimson hair was whipped by an eldritch wind, imbuing it with the disquieting aspect of a fiery halo, and her eyes blazed with an arcane radiance. I watched transfixed as the enchantress smiled mirthlessly and raised her staff, whereupon it disgorged a shrieking tendril of viridescent sorcery which smote a trio of enraptured Niaughu instantly to charred and riven ruin. I rose from the dank verdure and dragged my sword free of its scabbard as one of Nesadomntha's batrachian aberrations turned its malefic eyes upon me.

"The veil is lifted!" I bellowed to the shadowed form of Asenthine. "Now, deal red slaughter unto the thralls of the mound!"

The battle was joined and carnage reigned untrammelled. My sword clove into the leering mien of a shrieking Niaughu and split its vile, tentacled skull asunder. Greenish blood spattered my cuirass and I felt the opiate surge of power as the soul of the wretched creature surrendered to my enchantment's ravening hunger. In a searing blaze of icy light, the mystic armour of the Cosmic Ice abruptly manifested about me, shimmering and writhing upon my body like an undulating, spectral shell. Three more of the abominations fell before my steel like wheat before the scythe, and with each stroke I sensed my ensorcelled armour growing ever more engorged with eldritch might, the azure mana rapidly encasing my earthly form like a lucent chrysalis. All about me, the hulking sentinels of D'vartha solemnly engaged the keening fiends of the mound, and with a sense of grim satisfaction I realized that the miry warriors were indeed well matched against the foul vassals of Nesadomntha. I swept the misshapen head of a Niaughu from its sinewy body and spun to drive my befouled blade into the chest of another demon at my back. Thrice more my cerulean sword performed its butcher's work and a twisted pile of ravaged flesh and mangled limbs began to form at my feet.

I glanced to my left to see Asenthine performing a silent and elegant dance of slaughter amidst the throng of Niaughu, his slender blade weaving a scintillant web of pitiless death in the half-light. At the perimeter of the marsh, the adamantine hooves of Wrathmane struck like ice-bound hammers, dashing the skulls of any Niaughu who deigned to assail him into a foul slurry of green gore. A group of four crimson-eyed fiends then leapt toward me from the shadows of the swamp and pressed their ferine assault. One of the creatures attempted to sink its razor-edged fangs into my neck, but the cold steel of my gorget thwarted its attack and my blade dealt a ruinous blow in retaliation. My iron gauntlet shattered the distended jaw of the second devil just as the third pounced upon my shoulders and strove to wrest free my crested helmet. Instantly, I seized hold of the Niaughu's cranial tentacles and wrenched the beast from me, hurling it into the mire whereupon it was torn asunder by one of D'vartha's hulking marsh-men. The fourth fiend bared its acerose teeth and surged headlong at me, but the point of my sword was there to meet it, the blade punching through the vampyre's sternum and out through its serrated spine.

A deafening sound akin to a thunderclap then drew my attention and I glanced toward the barrow to see D'vartha unleashing a ruinous volley of sorcerous power from her gnarled staff. A score of Niaughu were reduced instantly to blackened husks by the coruscant energy and the witch then proceeded to disgorge another tendril of arcane power directly into the vine-wreathed mound. A gaping fissure opened instantly in the barrow's surface and like a crimson spectre, D'vartha swiftly disappeared beyond the blackened threshold of the aperture.

"She's ventured into that accursed sanctum to face Esmadrunga!" I bellowed to Asenthine.

The Alunai swordsman dragged his blade free of a Niaughu throat and turned his pallid, blood-spattered face to me. "But where is Nesadomntha? We must despatch that devil, or all is lost!"

I spun to the shadowed barrow to behold a seemingly ceaseless throng of Niaughu fiends issuing forth from the aphotic tunnel which brooded at the mound's base. Although we had thus far cut a glorious swath through the legions of the undead, many of the witch's miry myrmidons had fallen and it was clear that if Nesadomntha's hordes continued to be bolstered from the subterranean spawning-pit, the sheer weight of numbers would ultimately shift the balance of battle irrevocably against us.

"D'vartha will stem this vile tide!" I thundered. "We need only stand firm until her work is done, then the necromancer will be ours!"

An ominous and sepulchral growl like rolling thunder then rose above the cacophony of the battle and I descried a colossal black form begin to emerge slowly from the stygian tunnel. The mighty panther Sabarium crept malevolently forth, its iron muscles rippling beneath its sable fur, its vast scimitar fangs dripping with viscid saliva. The beast's single baleful eye glimmered like an emerald, while its other ruined socket still bore the grisly scar wrought by

Asenthine's blade. The great cat lowered its huge head and fixed its baleful gaze upon us, languorously stalking its prey like some pitiless hunter of distant prehistory.

Asenthine's cold eyes narrowed. "The odds grow increasingly against us, Karnov."

I hefted my imbrued blade reverentially. "Then let us strive to even them… by the strength of our sword-arms and the blistering kiss of our steel!"

Chapter IV
When Ferine Titans Clash (The Battle of the Marsh: Part II)

The conflagrant battle raged on, the marsh now ensanguined and choked with the sundered remnants of vampyric fiends and vanquished swamp golems. The legions of Niaughu were massing and inexorably beginning to overwhelm D'vartha's implacable, moss-encrusted horde. And yet the dwindling ranks of the miry sentinels stood firm and defiant, silently withstanding wave after wave of the ferocious vampyric assault like an immovable and verdant cliff-face defying the ceaseless crashing of a squamous sea. My indomitable steed Wrathmane continued to wreak his pitiless equine wrath upon any creature who dared to stand against him, his might bolstered inestimably by the same enchantment which even now filled my ensorcelled thews with unparalleled strength. Some yards distant, Asenthine calmly dispatched a trio of misshapen batrachian grotesqueries, his eyes grimly fixed on the slowly advancing war-panther Sabarium.

"It will take both of us to bring that thing down," I growled. "It's as big as an aurochs!"

"I think it bears me a grudge," replied Asenthine. "Well, I'll carve a few more pieces out of that black devil before it gets its claws into me, I swear it!"

Half a dozen Niaughu suddenly surged shrieking from the shadows. My sword dispatched two with a single stroke and I hammered my gauntlet into the face of the third, shattering the fiend's skull like an overly ripened melon. Roaring a battle-cry, I swept my radiant sword out in a mighty arc, the arcane steel shearing through the ribcage of the fifth creature before hacking into the neck of the sixth, sending its tentacled head spiralling through the air amidst a shower of feculent blood. Wiping foul ichor from my eyes, I glanced to where the embattled Asenthine stood and noted that the beast Sabarium had effortlessly cut down three marsh-men with primal savagery and was now crouched a mere six feet from the Alunai swordsman, poised to spring upon his nemesis and once more pit claw and fang against cold, hard steel. Before I could reach the nobleman's side, another screeching pack of Niaughu bolted from the morass to assail me. As my crackling steel met the fiends, I beheld the bitumen panther pounce, its fearsome jaws agape. At that moment, a great shadow suddenly seemed to obscure the lambent moon. Dragging my blade free of a Niaughu's cloven chest, I swiftly cast my gaze skywards to see a colossal black form swooping from the heavens, its vast leathern wings splayed like those of a gargantuan bat. With the force of an atramentous thunderbolt, the mist-wreathed shadow made landfall, brutally smiting Sabarium and sending the great cat reeling across the marsh. A heartbeat later, the astonished Asenthine spun to face his night-cloaked saviour.

"Merklethenon!"

The monstrous winged elk raised its head and gave vent to a deafening roar, its eyes aglow like rutilant embers. Abruptly, there sounded a resonant growl in response and Merklethenon wheeled his great cervine body to face Sabarium. The fearsome cat stalked slowly from the shadows, its baleful face contorted into a mask of ferine hatred. The two mighty beasts then began to circle one another at the centre of the benighted battlefield, their iron muscles shifting and rippling like black mercury.

"In truth, I thought we'd seen the last of your fell steed!" I called to Asenthine.

A grim smile crossed the swordsman's face. "I thank the Seven Avatars of the Alunai that he found his way back to me!"

The Niaughu fiends thronging the marsh began to fall back from the bizarre confrontation, giving the beasts ample space to wage their preternatural battle. Like two savage statues born of hoary myth and imbued with sinister life, Merklethenon and Sabarium eyed each other guardedly, their colossal bodies pulsing and heaving as if animated by the unerring hand of some otherworldly artisan. Then, uttering a stentorian roar, Sabarium pounced, his adamantine claws glimmering murderously in the moonlight. Merklethenon instantly lowered his head, brandishing his jagged antlers and meeting the great cat's powerful attack. Dragging my gaze from the primal duel of titans, I hammered my sword down into the flesh of a hissing Niaughu, cleaving the creature cleanly from its collarbone to its hip. From the reeking mire, another group of devils rushed headlong at me, their charge duly met by my unyielding steel. Nearly all of D'vartha's swamp golems had now fallen to the overwhelming might of the vampyric hordes, and yet the great barrow continued to disgorge an unending throng of the foul aberrations. In the midst of that desperate battle, I grinned wolfishly, for I knew that every Niaughu which fell before my sword only served to bolster my eldritch might. My rune-etched raiment was ablaze with cerulean light, its ceaselessly burgeoning luminosity casting a fulgent glow across the charnel-marsh, the sigils engraved into its surface burning like spectral beacons. So potent had the ghostly aura become that the flesh of any fiend who made contact with me was now immediately seared by the terrible, preternatural cold which my armour radiated. I had never before experienced power of this magnitude, and as I continued to carve a blood-sodden path through the multitudes, I found myself wondering if indeed there was any limit to the arcane might of the enchantment.

"Come, devils!" I bellowed exultantly. "Come and slake my ceaseless thirst! I shall smite and slay until not one of you stands, and only twisted flesh and sundered bones shall remain in my ruinous wake!"

"I'm glad you're enjoying yourself," barked Asenthine as he calmly dispatched another adversary. "But not all of us have the benefit of your ensorcelled vesture!"

"Fear not, Asenthine! If you fall in the fray, I shall battle on and avenge your death!"

"That was not my meaning," the Alunai hissed irately. "How

does the witch fare?"

"How should I know?" I gnarred, cleaving another Niaughu to mangled ruin.

"The spell she cast, you dolt!" Asenthine bellowed. "See through her eyes!"

"Ah, yes!" I replied. "In the grip of the red rage, I had all but forgotten!"

Immediately, I focused upon D'vartha, striving to picture the witch's alluring form in my mind's eye. To my astonishment, my field of vision instantly began to shimmer as the battleground's vista melted briskly away to be replaced by the subterranean tunnels of Esmadrunga's labyrinthine barrow. I was indeed seeing through D'vartha's eyes, presently beholding a charred and twisted mass of dead Niaughu in the torchlit cavern before me, evidently dispatched by the witch's sorcery. Moments later, another image coalesced in the shadow; that of the tentacled and tumescent form of Esmadrunga herself. I felt a shudder of revulsion as I gazed upon that familiar and disquieting entity; its pallid, moss-encrusted bulk shuddering obscenely in the slime-befouled depths and its vile, vaguely porcine countenance leering malevolently. I witnessed D'vartha's staff blaze abruptly with viridescent light, the sudden luminescence filling the foul subterrane with a scintillant and purifying aura. Instantly, the black eyes of Esmadrunga glimmered and her toothsome maw yawned wide. I continued to watch enthralled as D'vartha swiftly proffered the severed head of Xycanthia to the demonic queen, placing it reverentially within that viscid, pulsating orifice. A scant second before Esmadrunga's dagger-like teeth closed about the decaying skull, Xycanthia's dead eyes turned suddenly to behold her sister, the malefic orbs flaring brightly with a fell, crimson light. A ghastly, ululating scream then escaped the slain vampyress' rotting throat and a heartbeat later, the grotesquely bloated monarch of the mound promptly devoured the feculent offering whole. The image within the barrow then became shrouded in shadow and for a fleeting moment I was overcome with a sensation akin to falling from a precipitous height. With a jolt, my vision abruptly shifted to the marshy battleground once more.

"Well?" snapped Asenthine tersely.

"She has communed with Esmadrunga," I replied, feeling a sharp pain lance suddenly through my temples. "But there was no sign of Nesadomntha!"

"Then we fight on, and pray that witch's exploits have wrought something worthwhile!"

A deafening, bestial howl crested the tumult of the battle and I turned swiftly to behold the ongoing struggle between Merklethenon and Sabarium. Both of the primeval vampyric behemoths had evidently suffered grievous wounds during the course of the savage conflagration. The panther's ebony hide was riddled with deep gashes and the flanks of the mighty elk were likewise scored with a latticework of red furrows. With a final, guttural roar, Sabarium splayed his ensanguined scimitar-claws and leaped, his mighty muscles propelling him toward his adversary like a razor-fanged shadow. The dread claws of the night-cat duly tore six direful lacerations in the leathern wings of the black elk, but with a desperate lunge, Merklethenon succeeded in driving his twisted antlers deep into the panther's unprotected abdomen. A torrent of blood spattered the elk's muzzle and shoulders as the myriad needle-sharp points of those vile horns clove through the cat's steely muscles and sinew. A heartbeat later, Sabarium's lifeless frame crashed to the gore-choked mire and Merklethenon threw back his blood-sodden head to bellow his victory to the heavens.

"The beast is slain!" thundered Asenthine, his eyes agleam with exultation.

"But the hordes still come!" I replied. "There is no end to this madness!"

I stood now back-to-back with the Alunai swordsman, our steel glimmering like a radiant atoll in the midst of an aphotic sea. My searing shell of phantom-armour blazed with an effulgence so powerful that the legions of Niaughu surrounding us were evidently loath to press their attack, their bestial bloodlust clearly tempered by stark fear of the blistering magicks of my frozen steel. Casting my gaze across the mire, I noted grimly that the last of the stoic swamp golems had finally succumbed to the vampyric onslaught. The bloodied Merklethenon stood some yards distant, steadfastly keeping at bay a pack of batrachian fiends, while to my left I spied the azure form of Wrathmane moving slowly to our position, his searing hooves cutting a swathe through the Niaughu throng.

"This will be our last stand," I hissed to Asenthine. "I will fight on until they overwhelm me, or until my enchantment is depleted."

"How long can your ghost-armour endure?"

"The answer to that is unknown to me," I growled. "But at any rate, against such a horde as this… I fear we may fall before the sun rises."

The seething ring of Niaughu slowly began to press in upon us, their rutilant eyes sparkling balefully in the gloom. My cerulean sword pulsed and thrummed with eldritch energy as they crept closer, its gleaming aura illuminating the vile, distended faces of the undead horde.

Asenthine nodded solemnly. "Then let us make it a death worthy of legend!"

Suddenly, a powerful tremor shook the marsh, causing the mire to tremble and churn. Instantly, a blinding viridescent light blazed from the great mound of Esmadrunga, its source evidently the labyrinthine network of tunnels deep beneath the swamp. With an earsplitting din louder than any thunderclap, the lucent green corona exploded from the barrow's moss-encrusted surface and surged forth in a scintillant wave, engulfing the throngs of Niaughu in an immolating storm. Every fiend touched by that purifying nimbus was instantly blistered and burned, their flesh seared pitilessly from their bones and the remnants briskly reduced to little more than cinereal ash. Swiftly, the viridian light dissipated, leaving only charred and lifeless husks in its wake and a preternatural silence which brooded over the ensanguined mire. Lowering my sword, I glanced at the barrow to behold D'vartha emerging slowly from the tunnel at its base. A sardonic smile curled the witch's lips as she hefted her staff and strode purposefully toward us, her crimson tresses entangled with moss and leaves.

"I gather your covenant with the queen of the mound proved fruitful?" I enquired as she approached.

D'vartha regarded me quizzically for a moment before replying. "Esmadrunga? Ah yes, she was most vexed by her enthrallment. Once the spell which shackled her was broken, she chose to rid the world of her ill-spawned brood."

"And what of Nesadomntha?" snapped Asenthine. "Where is that depraved devil?"

D'vartha's eyes narrowed. "I did not encounter him in the depths. I found only the Niaughu and a score of the necromancer's cultists."

Asenthine's face instantly became a mask of bitter anger. "Damn that accursed bastard to the Thirteen Hells!"

As if in response to the Alunai's malediction, a great cloud of writhing black smoke abruptly manifested atop the mound. The stygian mass of fog pulsed and roiled for a moment before rising slowly into the night air, whereupon a familiar shape became visible within the undulating mist.

"Nesadomntha!" hissed Asenthine, brandishing his rapier.

The necromancer glared at us from the centre of the noisome maelstrom, his eyes ablaze with a fathomless hatred. "Deluded fools!" he rasped. "Revel in this hollow victory if you must, but know that you have thwarted merely one facet of my grand ambition!"

"Ha!" I roared. "Your foul vassals shall not overrun the land! We have sent them back to the black limbo from whence they came!"

Nesadomntha cackled derisively, his great braided moustache awhirl. "Pathetic defenders of humanity! Mankind is a plague upon the face of creation! If left unchecked, his virulence shall one day render this world a blackened husk… a barren and blighted purgatory! Only the embrace of death can avert this prophesied fate! The world must be cast to ruin, and once it has fallen, it shall be remade by my hand, a new genesis hewn to my own masterful design!"

"You're a madman!" snapped Asenthine.

"Mayhap," the necromancer whispered. "But as your proud Alunai race fell, so shall fall the race of Man! His citadels shall be razed to the ground, his armies shall be hammered into the dust! And those who survive the great purge shall be rendered malleable and all too willing to submit to the glorious dominion of Nesadomntha!"

"Such lunacy shall never come to pass!" I shouted. "Not by your hand, nor by the resurrection of your dead overlord!"

"Ghormanteia?" spat the necromancer with palpable disdain. "His vision was limited and his hubris unparalleled. In truth, I owe you a great debt for despatching him. I toiled in his servitude merely to learn his arcane secrets, all the while plotting to overthrow him when the opportunity arose. My treachery was a hundred years in the making! Those witless acolytes who even now strive for his rebirth shall ultimately bend the knee to me, for I shall rule supreme over man and vampyre alike, a divine god-king enthroned atop a charnel-mountain of the dead!"

"I have heard enough!" I thundered, hefting my numinous blade. "Come then! Pit your sorcery against my steel for the fate of the world, if you dare!"

Cruel laughter welled suddenly in the necromancer's throat. "I think not! I shan't debase myself by engaging vermin such as you! Seek me if you must, manling, but know that I cannot be vanquished! My glorious destiny is etched in the very firmament itself!" And with his voluminous sable cloak billowing as if it were an extension of the mist which entwined him, Nesadomntha uttered an incantation in a tongue unknown to me before lifting his twisted staff and disappearing abruptly from our sight like a spectral apparition.

"He has eluded us!" exclaimed Asenthine.

I lowered my sword sullenly. "We will pursue him."

"But how will we ascertain his destination?"

I turned to D'vartha. "Can your magicks track that villain through the void?"

The witch's brow furrowed momentarily. "I… believe so. Give me… a moment."

"Do not tarry!" barked Asenthine, moving briskly to Merklethenon's side. "We must give chase at once!"

I regarded D'vartha closely. Something about her manner seemed odd, but I deemed her fey demeanour to be attributable to the rigours of the recent battle. Whispering an oath and doffing my helmet, I strode to where my steed Wrathmane waited. His chanfron and peytral were slick with the green ichors of the Niaughu, but thankfully he bore no serious wounds from the fray.

"Merklethenon has suffered grievous injury," I heard Asenthine enounce behind me. "He may not be able to take to the skies until healed by the blood of a living creature."

"Then find him a rat or a lizard to sup on," I growled. "But do not deign to offer up an innocent human to the beast."

"You know I would not be so base," snapped the Alunai irately.

"Yes, what a nefarious deed that would be," whispered D'vartha, a strangely cold edge to her tone. "A vampyre daring to feed upon a human. How repugnant. How perfidious. One could almost deem it an aberration of nature."

"Do spare us your keen wit, D'vartha," I grumbled as I removed my azure gauntlets and adjusted the cinch strap of Wrathmane's saddle. "Kindly set to your task of locating the necromancer."

"What an onerous burden you bear, my dear Karnov," the witch continued, her voice now noticeably tinged with contempt. "You, who have dedicated your life to ridding the world of the vampyric scourge, burning with your righteous rage and bloated with such sanctimonious resolve."

I tensed imperceptibly as I heard the sorceress approaching me through the mire. Although I did not turn to face her, my hand fell swiftly to the leather pouch at my belt.

"Yes, what a thorny conundrum indeed," hissed D'vartha. "How full of self-loathing you must be, wielding your vaunted enchantment which drains the souls from the hated undead. Is such irony lost on you, Karnov? For in truth, what are you if not a vampyre yourself?"

I whirled an instant before D'vartha's dagger plunged into the base of my skull. Acting instinctively, I wrenched the blade from her grasp, holding her slender wrist in an iron grip. The witch snarled ferociously, her green eyes ablaze with a malefic rage. Swiftly, I pressed to her forehead the sapphirean gem given to me by Hegumen Hordane the Hierophant. D'vartha struggled desperately, shrieking in pain as the crystal made contact with her alabastrine flesh.

Staring directly into the woman's fever-bright eyes, I bellowed with untrammelled fury, "Get the hell out of my witch, *Xycanthia!*"

The crystal flared suddenly with a blinding radiance, and for a fleeting moment, D'vartha's body tensed. Then, with a great shuddering exhalation she fell limply into my arms. I withdrew the jewel from her brow and inspected it. The small stone's sapphirean hue had faded and it now resembled a shard of darkling obsidian. Additionally, it was strangely warm to the touch. Casting the tainted gem aside, I felt for D'vartha's pulse and was relieved to find it strong and steady.

A moment later, Asenthine appeared at my side, his rapier

poised. “What diabolism is this?” he hissed.

“Her beloved sister’s final act of treachery,” I muttered sullenly. “Make ready, Asenthine, we’re leaving this blighted mire!”

Chapter V
The Search for Nesadomntha Begins

D'vartha slowly regained consciousness and fixed me with a bone-weary gaze. "Where am I?" she whispered.

"A place of safety," I replied, brushing a lock of crimson hair from her emerald eyes.

Two hours ago, I had utilized the mystic transference powers of the Cosmic Ice to evacuate my allies from the accursed marsh of Kharag-Ghul, etching the lambent sigils which would open a portal between earthly locales. I had been able to effortlessly transport the entire party to safety, such was the magnitude of the energy I had absorbed from the multitudes of slain Niaughu. Swiftly bearing the insensate form of D'vartha to an abandoned crofter's hut in the moorlands of Duros Zuil, I had placed her upon a ramshackle pallet bed within the dilapidated structure and patiently awaited her recovery.

The witch's eyes abruptly widened in panic. "Xycanthia!"

"She is gone," I assured her. "I banished that vile soul from your body. The Hierophant of the Order of Mirkrash gifted me an arcane jewel before our departure from his realm. I'll wager that wily old sod suspected more than he cared to divulge."

D'vartha sighed with heartfelt relief. "Ah, my dear sister. Her spirit awakened mere seconds before Esmadrunga devoured her earthly remains. I felt her enter my mind, her power no doubt bolstered by Nesadomntha's necromantic influence within that corrupted sanctum."

I nodded. "I surmised as much, in truth."

"It was all I could do to keep her spirit from consuming me completely," the witch stammered. "The struggle was dire. Her hatred for you was so powerful. I tried to stop her…"

"It is done," I muttered. "Her malign soul now wanders the Outer Darkness, where it shall remain forevermore."

"I pray you are right. Twice now has my mind been supplanted by another... my flesh serving as a vessel for a malefic consciousness. I vow it shall never happen again!"

"That's an oath well sworn, lass!"

A wry smile then curled D'vartha's lips. "It seems I needed your assistance after all, Karnov."

My brow arched wryly. "It must truly have pained you to admit that."

"Aye, well, don't get used to it," the witch scowled.

"Can you divine the whereabouts of Nesadomntha?" I asked. "Asenthine and I have made a pact to hunt down that elusive necromancer."

"Yes," the witch replied, rising unsteadily from the crude bed. "And I shall accompany you on your quest. I have no desire to return to my arcane garden. Not after the vile taint which my sister placed upon it, at any rate."

"I... *we* would welcome your company," I grumbled.

D'vartha suddenly gripped my hand, her face a mask of grave concern. "You mean to slay Asenthine, do you not?" she whispered tensely. "Once the threat of Nesadomntha has been dealt with?"

My brow furrowed in vexation. "You know me too well, witch. I am oath-bound to purge the land of the undead. It matters not that he claims to hail from a race of benevolent vampyres. In truth, I scarcely believe such things are possible. Asenthine and I shall have our reckoning. But I will strive to ensure that our final battle is fair."

"And then you shall seek to discover the secrets of the Cosmic Ice, guided by the dream of which you spoke?"

"I shall."

D'vartha sighed sorrowfully, her eyes downcast. "Know that I will not be able to accompany you on that journey, Karnov. That quest is for you alone to undertake. I only pray that you are prepared for the revelations which await you."

I moved to the ruined door of the hut, taking up my gently glowing helmet from a broken trestle table. With a start, I suddenly spied my reflection in a broken looking glass which hung adjacent to the door frame. The face which stared back at me from the depths of the tarnished mirror was gaunt and weary. The pale blue eyes were grim and shadowed with a profound solemnity, and the once ebon beard was now shot through with streaks of grey. I sighed, acknowledging the ruinous toll which the previous several years had exacted upon both my spirit and my flesh. The man I once was had perished; he had died alongside his beloved wife and son. In his place was something stronger, more pitiless, and inestimably darker of soul. Such was the price of my enduring vow and the power which accompanied it… and it was a heavy price indeed. Gathering my thoughts, I donned my helmet and turned back to D'vartha. "Join us when you are ready."

The first light of dawn was colouring the eastern horizon as I strode to the rotting wooden fence where my steed Wrathmane was tethered. Glancing to the broad, rock-strewn trail which fronted the hut, I descried Asenthine and Merklethenon, their gaze fixed upon the rising sun. The ravaged carcasses of three sheep were strewn at the black elk's feet and his great muzzle was bright with blood.

"I do wish you'd keep that beast out of sight," I growled. "If anybody chances to lay eyes upon it, we'll have the militias of every duchy in the land hot on our heels."

Asenthine turned to face me, his eyes agleam in the dawn light. "Can she track the necromancer?"

"Yes," I replied.

"Nesadomntha will not escape us," the Alunai whispered gravely. "He shall fall, and when I have his head, I shall hunt down the acolytes of the slain Ghormanteia and put them to the sword. No vestige of that foul cult must remain. Such is my vow, Karnov."

"And it is a vow I share," I replied. "Ghormanteia shall never rise again. His black soul was devoured by my enchantment and his remaining vassals shall be cut from the land like gangrenous flesh from a diseased limb."

Asenthine's cold eyes remained fixed on me as he secured his rapier in its ornate scabbard. "Any who stand in my way will perish, human."

My hand moved imperceptibly closer to the icy hilt of my sword. "I believe we understand each other, Asenthine."

D'vartha then emerged swiftly from the shadowed hut, leaning upon her gnarled staff. "East!" she declared. "Nesadomntha has fled to his sanctum in the black necropolis which sprawls at the heart of Khefra Zuil. There he waits amongst the ancient pyramidal tombs of the great desert… in the Valley of the Deathless Kings!"

"Can your power transport us to that distant realm, Karnov?" asked Asenthine tensely.

"Let us find out," I growled, preparing to drag my sword from its scabbard.

"It would avail you naught!" exclaimed D'vartha. "The realm of Khefra Zuil is a nexus between the worlds of the living and the dead. It broods beneath the aegis of the Hieroglyphs of Neterkhertet, the power of which thwarts even the sorcery of the Cosmic Ice!"

Asenthine and I exchanged pensive glances. Then, without a word, the Alunai swordsman deftly mounted the replete Merklethenon and wheeled the great elk on to the broad trail. Swiftly, I lifted D'vartha to Wrathmane's back and climbed into the saddle. "Onwards, then!" I bellowed exultantly. "Once more into the embrace of battle to deal red ruin and searing slaughter unto the vile thralls of darkness!"

And we rode east towards the rising sun.

Perilous indeed was Karnov's journey into the sand-flayed realms of the eastern pharaohs, but at length he and his stead-

fast companions stood resolutely before the great cyclopean sanctum of the mad necromancer Nesadomntha. The black horrors which they encountered in that desolate domain were myriad, and the vile secrets uncovered within the hoary catacombs of the Deathless Kings were enough to rend a man's mind and sear his very soul. But that is another story…

Afterword

Eyes of the screech owl glow deep in the night
Like skull-mounted candles ablaze
A phantom-clad rider spreads eerie ghost-light
His spectral sword raging in flames
From out of their lairs vampire slave-girls return
Eager mouths for their gift-bearing lord
Among poison lichens and black lotus ferns
They kneel as the lifeblood is poured

I wrote these lines a few years ago for the opening verse of an Eternal Winter song entitled "In the Nightside of the Forest Black." The lyrics were written simply to create a Gothic atmosphere, and had no specific meaning at the time.

A year or two later, while organizing material for the Majestic Metal Records release *Bloodmist At Dawn* (a compilation album featuring heavy metal songs by bands of Sword and Sorcery authors), I began reading a book called *Ghor, Kin-slayer.* This novella, originally written in 1979, consisted of several fairly well-known fantasy writers taking an unfinished Robert E. Howard tale and running with it—each contributing a chapter where the previous author left off. While I liked the book, the most intriguing aspect of it to me was how each writer added their own unique touch to the story, and how they creatively dealt with the conflicts created by the author that preceded them.

An idea struck me to organize a similar collaboration but on a smaller (and perhaps neater) scale. I presented it to my two friends and heavy metal fantasist brothers-in-arms, Byron A. Roberts and Howie K. Bentley. They were both genuinely excited and agreed on the spot to be a part of it. We were all ready to begin writing but there were two obstacles to overcome—what was the story going to be about, and what order would we go in? Eventually, I volunteered to go first and started brainstorming on some things to write about. I wanted to come up with a good beginning plot, and above all, a strong main character. I thought of an idea to do something with a 'sword and sorcery meets Hammer Films' kind of vibe. I started going through material I had previously written to see if I had something unfinished that might suffice. In my archives of old, handwritten drafts, I happened to come across the song lyrics for "Nightside" which I mentioned above. The opening lines jumped right out at me, and I instantly had a vision of a phantom-clad rider who fought vampires. I soon developed an idea for a main character, and an opening plot started materializing in my mind. Once I had written the first draft of Episode I, I passed it on to Howie who then began his installment. Once that was complete, he forwarded both Books onto Byron who had the task of penning the epic conclusion.

When all was finalized, we were quite happy with the first story. We thought it was a great tale that flowed nicely, and very importantly—the 'voice' and style of each author shone through just as we were hoping. Since the three of us all agreed the story turned out well, we started throwing around ideas to have it published. We eventually decided that rather than submitting to various anthologies or magazines, it would be a good idea to write an additional episode in order to compile a full novel. We dove back into the world of Karnov head-first, and soon Karnov's second adventure was underway.

The result of this great collaboration has exceeded my wildest expectations, and I couldn't be happier with the final product! When I read this epic, round-robin novel in its entirety, I am captivated by the amount of blood-fueled action, tragic drama, vibrant imagery, humor, unique, memorable characters, and clever, Screaming for Vengeance storyline that's sure to please any fan of dark fantasy. I feel honored to have worked with these two brilliant authors, and I hope that all the readers of this book have enjoyed our creation as much as I do.

By the Severed Head of Ghormanteia,
Matthew Knight
Summer, 2019

ALSO AVAILABLE

Want to get an e-book for free? *The Infernal Bargain and Other Stories* is available exclusively for DMR Books mailing list subscribers. Go to https://dmrbooks.com/ and get your copy now!

The Chronicles of Caylen-Tor by Byron A. Roberts – The Wolf-King of the north, Caylen-Tor, does battle with imperial armies and sorcerous serpent-men in three exciting novellas! Spectacular sword-and-sorcery by the lyricist of Bal-Sagoth.

Swords of Steel Omnibus – *Swords of Steel,* with its novel concept of fantasy stories written by members of heavy metal bands, was the most critically-acclaimed sword-and-sorcery anthology series of recent years. Now every story from all three volumes is packaged together! Features Howie Bentley (Cauldron Born), Byron Roberts (Bal-Sagoth), E.C. Hellwell (Manilla Road), Mike Scalzi (Slough Feg) and many more.

Lands of the Earthquake by Henry Kuttner/Under a Dim Blue Sun by Howie K. Bentley – The first split release from DMR Books in the tradition of the Ace Double series! *Lands of the Earthquake* is a classic science-fantasy adventure from the pulp era that has never been published in book form before. On the flip side you'll find a brand new sword-and-planet tale. A US soldier hijacks a Nazi spaceship and lands on a planet threatened by snake-men! This title is available exclusively from DMRBooks.com.

Death Dealers & Diabolists – Eight action-packed tales of swords and sorcery! Includes stories by Keith Taylor (author of the *Bard* series) and Buzz Dixon (writer for *Thundarr the Barbarian, G.I. Joe* and *Transformers).*

Printed in Great Britain
by Amazon

62653564R00123